THE TIME OF THE KINGFISHERS

The Time of the KINGFISHERS

DAVID WATMOUGH

ARSENAL PULP PRESS

VANCOUVER

THE TIME OF THE KINGFISHERS

ARSENAL PULP PRESS
100-1062 Homer Street
Vancouver, B.C.
Canada V6B 2W9

The publisher gratefully acknowledges the assistance of the Canada Council and the Cultural Services Branch, B.C. Ministry of Small Business, Tourism and Culture.

Cover design by Gek-Bee Siow
Cover photograph of Floyd St. Clair and David Watmough courtesy of David Watmough
Printed and bound in Canada by Kromar Printing

CANADIAN CATALOGUING IN PUBLICATION DATA:
Watmough, David, 1926-
The time of the kingfishers

ISBN 1-55152-008-7
I. Title.
PS8595.A8T5 1994 C813'.54 C94-910730-1
PR9199.3.W37T5 1994

AUTHOR'S STATEMENT

≈

During two decades of publishing fiction, I have been meted some extraordinary experiences. My first would-be editor committed suicide in New York during a violent storm that blew my novel's pages all over Greenwich Village. A Toronto publisher of a later book went bankrupt, a third dropped my manuscript into Lake Ontario, and a fourth proved a crook. But far outstripping all these events have been the incidents attending the publication of this present novel. It began life under the title *Families* and subsequent to its publisher being accused of sexual harrassment by one of her male employees, she departed the publishing business. So *Families* only amounted to a carton of copies with the remainder, I suspect, being shredded by irate and unpaid printers. The manuscript was then taken over from scratch by a Toronto publishing house and, with further revisions, a handsomely designed cover, and a new title, *The Time of the Kingfishers*, was scheduled for publication in the spring of 1994 before once more suffering a last-minute abortion. Now, however, one of the most proofread novels in history is finally seeing the light of published day, and I confess that it is not pride and satisfaction but relief which consumes me after a protracted gestation of six years.

—David Watmough
Vancouver

This novel is dedicated to my friends
John Hulcoop and Wayne McDermott
and Sally Hulcoop, and in cherished
memory of Adam Hulcoop.

"Now, every winter, the hen-kingfisher carries her dead mate with great wailing to his burial, and then, building a closely compacted nest from the thorns of the sea-needle, launches it on the sea, lays her eggs in it, and hatches out her chicks. She does all this in the Halcyon days—the seven which precede the winter solstice, and the seven which succeed it—while Aeolus forbids his winds to sweep across the waters."

—Robert Graves, *The Greek Myths*

PART ONE

ONE

I was about to celebrate my sixth birthday in Vancouver (my fortieth on the planet) when I met Gordon and Helen Goddard. Helen first and Gordon ten days later. It was a morning in late July and I was taking the ferry to Victoria to see a woman with whom I'd been in correspondence for—as a fellow Celt—she wished to write of us Cornish in British Columbia.

Helen was sitting alone on the white painted locker, as close to the prow of the ship as passengers were allowed. She was reading a Penguin novel. She appeared to be about my own age and wore her brown hair in a loose bun at the back of her neck. It was she who spoke first. I am invariably shy with strangers and excessively so with women. We had just entered Active Pass and instead of the ship's horn falling silent after its regular blast of warning, it continued to sound alarms to the impervious pleasure craft which blocked the ferry's way. Although she hadn't even looked up when I perched a few feet away from where she sat, Helen now addressed me. "Stupid idiots! They deserve to be swamped. They know bloody well the ferries work to schedule."

She still had an English accent. My own British background accorded her Outer London or at least south east England as hers. Her place back in that tight class structure we'd both left I put as "lower-middle." She might have started off as a nurse or an elementary schoolteacher, the sociological Sherlock Holmes in me decided. I was thrown a quick look by gray-green eyes. I saw I was expected to respond to her irate observation.

"They may be stupid, but it's the selfishness that gets me," I volunteered. That evidently pleased her for she closed her paperback with an emphatic snap.

"How right you are! Selfish bastards! They're just like those who drive through red lights or leave their empty bottles on the beach. Don't you think there's more of all that than there used to be? Or is it just Canada after England? You're from Britain, aren't you?"

We proceeded to swop pedigrees and, apart from learning her name, I discovered my social and geographic pigeon-holing was less than accurate. Helen was born in Frome, Somerset, the daughter of a Baptist minister, and had worked for the library until meeting her husband, Gordon, a post-office worker in Bristol. With their infant son, Derek, they'd decided to emigrate to Canada. After two Toronto winters they'd pushed on to the gentler climate of coastal British Columbia. She was on her way to a great-aunt who'd recently entered an old people's home. I had the impression she wasn't looking forward to seeing the old lady who'd homesteaded on the prairies, but she insisted on speaking positively about the visit.

Energy . . . ebullience . . . these were the attributes I associated with Helen from the start. And her uncompromising Englishry. It wasn't so much her reluctance to yield British terminology for North American usage. There was nothing of the petrol and lorry business about her, even if she was not as North Americanized as I was. Instead, her conversation was animated by a bubbly recall of things and places she'd long left behind.

Halfway along the coast of Galiano Island she pointed to the tall cliffs where Belted Kingfishers darted and dove, and asked whether the cliffs reminded me of Cheddar Gorge in Somerset. I said they did and that I also recalled kingfishers in Cornwall.

"I remember the kingfishers at Nunney Ketch outside of Frome, when I was a kid. Only they were much more beautiful than this lot," she added scornfully. "A brilliant blue with scarlet on their heads and lovely beige breasts. They looked as if they belonged to the Amazon or somewhere really exotic."

She looked wistful. Abruptly turned to the subject of very English sweets like "Malteezers," "jelly-babies" and "gob-stoppers." That led us into a litany of shared childhood memories of wartime 'blended' chocolate and how we'd carefully spent our 'personal points' allotted to candy rationing—which somehow brought us both to gales of laughter.

As a bonus, while the handsome blue-gray kingfishers still glided softly down the face of the cliff to the sparkling waters below, she threw in an hilarious imitation of the formal news bulletins of the BBC—read in tones of Cathedral solemnity.

Soon afterwards, she had to return to her bus and I to my car, but already we had established a bond between us. We agreed to meet again soon when back on the mainland.

I told Ken about meeting Helen when I got home and although he greeted my enthusiasm with his usual tolerance, he did warningly suggest that shipboard romances were often best left at sea. He had good reason to hold my ardour in check. Over the ten years of our relationship there'd been too many times when brief encounters of mine had led to newly made *friends* turning up who proved to be drunkards, pilferers, pathological liars—or sometimes all three!

When Helen duly called a few days later I felt not only justified over her serious intent but superstitiously confident my run of ill luck with *strangers-met-in-transit* was over. That feeling was reinforced when we arrived at the Goddards' West End apartment, been gushingly welcomed by Helen, and introduced to her equally affable husband, Gordon, and their sturdy but sleeping son, Derek.

To be harshly accurate, my recollection of that first of innumerable evenings which the four of us (plus Derek) spent in each other's company, is rather spotty. Then I am spanning the memories of over eighteen years. I do recall, though, a huge bouquet of flowers—reminiscent of those to be found on the counters of English pubs—adorning the dining room table. There was also the view.

In 1963 there were fewer high-rises in Vancouver's West End and the very tallest were to come much later. But the Goddards' building was high enough on a slope to grant a superb view of the waters towards distant Point Grey.

Looming more in significance, however, than apartment objects, or vistas was Gordon—a thin figure nervously counterpointing his wife's wit. Gordon Neville Goddard, we learned within minutes of our arrival, worked for the public relations department of the B.C. Telephone Company. He now wrote copy instead of answering night calls as a telephone operator for the British post office in Bristol.

I cottoned to him right off the bat—just as I had his wife. I was also pleased to see Kenneth chatting with Helen—though with his California background they couldn't chuckle over a common childhood in wartime England.

They soon discovered a mutual interest in such English novelists as George Eliot and Fielding. While I discussed San Francisco and New Jersey days with Gordon I overheard references to such characters as Dorothea Brooke and Jonathan Wild from the other two.

On that first day a very small boy was just a flushed face upon a pillow. I don't think we ever saw him asleep after that! On the way home in the car we discussed the Goddards. There were a couple of factors we found puzzling. The mystery was not to be resolved for several months but partial illumination came on the occasion of my birthday two weeks later.

We held the party in our minuscule backyard. Climber roses screened us from neighbours on either side. There was a buffet in the dining room and card tables and folding chairs scattered about the pocket lawn for the dozen guests.

Several friendships were forged that August evening and perhaps a couple of enmities. Henry Brent, a morose old queen who taught music in high school, had bitchy words with an equally saturnine drama teacher from one of the community colleges which had just come into being.

Their area of conflict centered on the talent—or lack of it—owned by the late Judy Garland. As their sarcastic nasalities were sneered over gin-and-tonics, Ken and I signalled each other with practised ease. Obese Henry Brent had been a last minute substitute for a woman biologist who'd been obliged to fly south to San Diego for the interment of a parent. The other—scrawny Sidney Evans—I'd met that spring at a drama conference and he proved to be one of my famous disasters. It was to be the last time Sidney entered our house.

All that, though, was just a minor buzz at the circumference of our activities. As old hands at bringing gaggles of gays together we were quite accustomed to the odd tiff and competitions in tartness—especially when the booze had blurred decorum and loosened the tongues of the nervous and self-conscious.

First to arrive (as always) was Ken's UBC colleague, diminutive Neil

Murphy and his pregnant French wife, the raven-haired Jacqueline. Although neither of them were churchgoers I'd promised to be godfather to whatever she was about to bring into the world. If previous party patterns were pursued this time, she would take the car and return to Point Grey before her husband. Neil would stay, drink more, and—if he made out—depart to the shared bed of any of our male guests who happened to be tolerably good-looking and complaisant.

I guess little Neil was what by the eighties had come to be known as 'bi'—but which back in the sixties we were prone to call 'AC/DC.' It wasn't a topic brought up readily in conversation with either Murphy.

Our four-way friendship was relaxed enough—with a lot of affection flowing between us. They rarely addressed the specifics of my living with Ken. This mutual reticence over labelling sexual liaisons was an easeful thing and came quite naturally to us, but it didn't prevent intimate confidences between the Latin-lively Jacqueline and me. After all, our men were both professors on campus: she and I felt the bonding of faculty wives. . . .

As we sauntered through the house to the back we were already deep in conversation about an incipient scandal between an aging professor in the English Department and one of his female graduate students who was incautiously prone to writing love-letters to the bearded old goat. Professor Weldon had already exhausted two wives and a mistress and raised a large brood of children but seemed anxious to again offer his run-down reproductive faculties to the human race.

Neil went to help Ken with the drinks. When Horace Weldon had been finally laid to filth by the two of us, Jacqueline nudged me and spoke quickly in her attractive French accent. "So when does your new girlfriend arrive? I am dying to meet the competition!"

I told her not to be silly, adding I felt sure they'd enjoy each other. That proved to be the case. One of the highlights of my fortieth birthday party was the forming of a firm alliance between the Goddards, the Murphys and us.

The Murphys were really *very* early—a good twenty minutes before the agreed time. I decided I'd drop a gentle hint to Master Neil, who in such domestic matters was less prickly than his spouse. The premature arrival, however, did provide us with an opportunity to talk intimately at a table in the arbour at the edge of the freshly mown lawn.

At first we spoke of Jacqueline's pregnancy which I found a fascinating topic. Every time we met that summer I begged her for an update on her condition—which she happily imparted with infinite detail. She was close to climaxing the process and her body was already thickened and her ankles swollen. She told me the heat we'd experienced in recent weeks had made her particularly irritable and that she and Neil had been quarreling more fiercely than usual. That didn't surprise me. The Murphys were frequently fractious and I was personally aware the heat-wave had shortened all our tempers.

To console her I spoke of a nasty row I had with Ken when I'd run out of the house and skulked and sulked in the darkened garden for an hour. We mocked my over-reaction to a minor domestic crisis and then she cited the time when she had poured three quarters of a bottle of Bushmill's whiskey down the sink because her husband, in his Irish insularity, had refused to eat the surprise gazpacho she had prepared.

Neil then joined us and Ken went to the front door to answer the bell and let in a whole bunch of guests who'd arrived at the same time. The talk became general.

Until the advent of Helen and Gordon Goddard, that is. After introducing Helen to Jacqueline I whisked my ferry acquaintance away for a quick tour of the house. Other than Ken—busy with pouring drinks—we encountered only fat Henry Brent who hovered, as usual, about the array of bottles on the kitchen counter. As this was before his spat with Sidney he was still reasonably sober though evil enough without alcoholic stimulus, to ask Helen if she'd been hired for the evening. Her reply was prompt. She told him 'no' firmly—but swiftly followed that up by claiming they'd met before at the opera when he'd been wearing a blonde wig, and a white rabbit-fur coat which had excited the delight of his entourage which had addressed him as Delilah.

With that she turned on her heels and, with me in her imperious wake, sailed out into the hallway and up the stairs. As I guided her in the direction of my study Helen loudly observed that Henry Brent was the kind of queen who always wanted to borrow her dance pumps when they wore drag and in doing so, ruined them.

I had the impression she was thoroughly familiar with the Henry Brents of this world. (Both Ken and I had noted, right from our first visit to the Goddards, that she had taken our own evident gay relationship for granted.) Shortly after that, as we stood behind my desk and peered down on the crowded garden scene, she confirmed just how conversant she was with our species, or at least one version of it.

"So you've met the likes of our Henry before," I commented casually, still looking down at my birthday guests. "He's such an old fart, I really don't know why we ask him year after year. Out of pity, I suppose."

"The trouble is," Helen said evenly, "he gives all gays a bad name. I spend *hours* telling the superintendent at our apartment building that some nice single men make super tenants—and then along comes a Henry who in two bitchy cracks can make me out a liar!"

I made no reply but took good care to memorize her revealing comments for Ken's ears later that night. The other incident involved her husband, when it was quite dark and a sole guttering candle was alone left to illumine people's features. The savage little exchange between Henry and Sidney had taken place and the latter had already left in a huff. Irene Halliwell, a lesbian landscape gardener, was snoring in a deck chair while her girlfriend, Eva, whom we'd not previously met, had commandeered the guest bed to pass out on. They were a fairly new relationship and I agreed with Ken when he suggested the excitement of meeting new people, and the quantities of drink nervously imbibed, had combined to collapse both of them.

Jacqueline had gone home, as predicted, taking the car. Her husband was arguing fiercely for nuclear disarmament—presumably with himself for he was sitting alone in the dark. I could make out Helen's head from the light of the kitchen window and concluded she was helping Ken clear up.

Gordon was talking to an only half-listening me as I debated whether I should leave him and go inside to help wash up dirty glasses.

"Do you like Vancouver?"

I looked at him, puzzled. "Of course. Why?"

He paused before replying. I had the feeling he was carefully picking his words. "What I really meant to say is do you know Vancouver very well?"

"I think so. You can test me if you like."

From then on he didn't prevaricate. "Know a place called Dino's?"

"You mean the steamers? You're interested in the tubs?"

"I'd just like to know what goes on in them. I—I've never had the courage to go to a steambath."

Until that moment I wasn't certain that Gordon was gay, although it explained why Helen was *au fait* with so much. I recalled Ken commenting that he felt the Murphys and the Goddards might have something in common in terms of their male components—however weird the coincidence that their lives should now converge with ours.

"They could prove a very useful institution—especially for the likes of me."

I sipped my scotch and soda. Gordon seemed in a confessional mood. I banished all thoughts of helping them inside. I was rarely disposed to refuse a confidence—provided it wasn't a confession.

"When you think of it, they really are a neat idea. I mean if it's possible to just slip down there and get your rocks off. After that I guess you could go home and do your stuff properly there."

That was something which mildly ruffled me. "I suppose it's possible Helen might be keen at times you have your rocks 'on,' as it were!"

He grimaced. "I'm not really talking about much more than the French businessman who visits his mistress on his way home to dinner."

That was a topic I felt needed the balance of two distinct viewpoints—but it was neither my duty nor my disposition at my own party to supply the opposing one. Instead, I gave Gordon the names of several pertinent establishments embellished by the subtle but distinct variations which the clientele of each embraced.

He nodded formally at each description I offered—as if I were briefing him on possible private schools for son Derek. (Both he and Helen had expressed dissatisfaction that evening with the school their boy was attending.)

I finally exhausted my catalogue of fleshly wares: the young crowd at the Mermaid, the older patrons of the Olympic, the hustlers in evidence at the Service Club. . . .

I'd only just finished when we were joined by Helen and Ken—fresh from their kitchen chores and ready for a nightcap. Neil now concluded his soliloquy on nuclear disarmament and when the rest came back into the garden, drew up his own chair more closely into the circle. Irene Halliwell, awaking suddenly, bid us all a cheerful if blurred good-night and staggered indoors to collect her comatose mate and drive their truck through suburbia to Fort Langley.

That left five of us sitting there, sipping our final drinks and staring up into the celestial morass of the Milky Way. On the warm summer air crickets chirped and once, between the desultory swish of late-night traffic, I thought I heard the high twitter of bats as they dived for moths and midges.

After a protracted silence Helen suddenly asked Neil if he and Jacqueline had yet decided upon a name for their child. Neil stirred uncomfortably. I knew very well that late in the evening, with a substantial amount of liquor in him, any kind of *familial reference* was unsettling, to say the least.

"She's probably decided, but I haven't played 'read my mind' with her yet."

"You mean you haven't even discussed it together? I can hardly believe that," said Helen. "Gordon and I had at least three flaming fights before agreeing on something as tame as 'Derek'—didn't we, dear? And I'm leaving out the rows over possible girls names before 'D' hove into sight with a tassel!"

"Thelma, Janice, even Hermione! Wasn't all *that* a waste of time," Gordon commented.

"I don't know. At least we agreed on no Janice—just in case it should ever come up again."

It was the very first time, I told myself, that I'd heard Helen sound even the faintest bit coy—with that reference to future possibilities. Coy or not, all she got in response from her mate was a loud snort.

"Are you kidding? Come up again? Not if I can fucking well help it!

My diaper-changing days are over. And I already feel our beloved son could do with at least two more sets of parents as back-up. God knows what he'll be like when he gets into his teens. You should have heard the screams tonight when he was left with his favourite baby-sitter. Spoiled little bugger!"

"One father who took some notice and shared some authority would be a help," Helen sighed affectedly. Then she turned to the rest of us in the semi-circle. "The trouble is, you see, our dear child is in danger of ending up with two *mothers.*"

Gordon was silent. Made no effort to defend himself. Neil was uncharacteristically quiet too. It was Ken who lanced the mood by suddenly looking up and crying out that he'd seen a shooting star.

"That means another baby is being born, doesn't it?" I asked rhetorically. "Although what *its* name will be and how many Mummies and Daddies he or she will have in its life I'm afraid we shall never know."

TWO

≈

Jacqueline wanted a dog, a puppy, to grow up with her baby when it came. She asked me to accompany her in visiting various kennels specializing in the breeds she had decided would be most suitable. When she invited me I was rather amused. Jacqueline was transparently Anglophile, unlike most of her compatriots, and this new 'dogginess' was only the latest Albion propensity—which already included a predilection for kippers, Marmite yeast extract, milk in her tea, and constant references to her Dublin-based mother-in-law as 'Mum.' (She had patently decided, on meeting Neil, to incorporate *Hiberniaphilia* into her general passion for the mores of the British Isles.)

Not surprisingly, as we set out on our canine expedition, the breeds she expressed interest in were Kerry Blue terriers and Irish and English setters. I think she would've included English bulldogs if it hadn't seemed so risibly obvious.

As she drove us I had the recurrent impression that the thrall of Anglophilia was also informing her driving. "We're not in Ireland or England now, darling, even if we are looking for a Kerry Blue. You're making that truck-driver rather cross."

She laughed. "You're a worse back seat driver than Neil! That guy's taking up too much of the highway. All those beer-bellied men are the same." She jutted her angular chin and I noted spots of irritation on her rather sallow cheeks. "When they see it's a woman driving they're grotesque. They think their balls are being threatened!"

I didn't point out the size of the man's belly was wholly hid from us and that he may have been a 7-Up addict for all we knew—with a stomach as flat as an ironing board.

I became distinctly more relaxed when we eventually reached the TransCanada with its several lanes affording her ample room for the Volkswagen.

"Ouch!" she exclaimed, as we sped towards New Westminster. "The little sod just kicked me!"

My bewilderment (increased by my sweat over her speed and

nervousness over her abhorrence of yellow lines) must've been immediately obvious.

"The *baby*," she explained. "He always lets me know when he wakes up. Any minute now he'll start to dance."

I glanced quickly at the blue cotton of her maternity dress where it stretched across her stomach. Then I stared at the pavement of the highway ahead of us. It wasn't her erratic driving which preoccupied me. I strove to picture the foetal activity inside my friend. I thought of her darkness and how different it must be from mine. If there was rapid change in the depth of me it probably spelled carcinogenic *death* whereas her atramentous interior was now geared finely to the prod toward *life*.

I couldn't bring even a tadpole to reality. The echo in my questing male imagination was only of tepid womb-water and blood. I thought savagely of the anti-abortionists—those bigots who blasphemously ignored the evolutionary miracle of the unfolding stages from egg to fish, to mammal and final human birth at a woman's breech, and whined their uneasy fear of nature's arcane mysteries and the allure of the holy dark.

I licked dry lips, suddenly restless with her pregnancy. "Can you tell when its wants to jive rather than waltz?" I asked.

The mother-to-be saw through my bluff. "Neil also gets upset when I mention his child. He's actually forbidden me to give him the gory details about what's happening. Coming from my baby's father I find that really sick. On the other hand—with a hardened bachelor like you. . . . " She actually took her gloved hands off the steering wheel to shrug.

"What you mean, Jacqueline, is you quite understand why a gay like me should get uptight about gynecological details but that *real* men like Neil shouldn't."

That got to her. "Are you just stubborn or really stupid? How many times do I have to tell you I *never* think of you in that way. I know you're gay, Davey, because you're always telling me so. I wouldn't necessarily have guessed had you not lived with Ken. You do not have the gay vibes."

I sniffed. "Vibes, Madame, doesn't need a definite article in English."

She made no reply. Jacqueline was sensitive about her English, even though she had little reason to be.

"Let's go to the Kerry Blue place first," she suggested crisply. "I had a peculiar conversation with the woman there. It might turn out the most interesting kennel. That's just from the human angle. Her dogs are well-known, too."

Well-known at dog shows, I told myself a few minutes later, but certainly concealed from the general public in Aldergrove. The place lay up a bumpy, unmade track behind a tall stand of poplars interspersed with clumps of willow. Beyond lay straggly fields with corrugated shacks in the corner of some and a general air of untidiness and neglect. It reminded me of the worst aspects of rural California.

I said as much to Jacqueline as we bumped along a rutted lane towards the still invisible kennels. "You can understand why the ecology movement is getting so big. There isn't much neatness, is there? These buildings are as much a pollution as the pesticides farmers use."

Jacqueline frowned. "That's part of the price one has to pay. Of course, when I married Neil I thought we'd be living in Dublin with a weekend cottage in Connemara. Or if he'd been teaching in an English redbrick, a charming little house in the country. But we ended up in Vancouver. We could've done worse. Imagine one of those dreadful places like Hamilton or Sudbury."

"But out here in the country should be so attractive," I argued. "It's always man who screws things up!"

We were slowing down. Now we were surrounded by rusting artifacts knee-high in undergrowth: a discarded fridge, a much dented oil drum, and the frame of a bicycle. Jacqueline switched off the ignition and we heard a din of barking dogs.

There was no one in sight. I think we were both affected by the atmosphere. The barks and yelps grew more incessant. I saw a dead robin, its feathers sodden, lying in the bramble-strewn verge. Over the commotion of the invisible dogs I heard the sound of what I first took to be sheep and then decided was a single goat.

As we clambered out of the VW the dog roar grew more frantic. "If that's Kerry Blues," I shouted, "you'd better try Chow-chows. They're supposed to be silent!"

Jacqueline playfully grabbed my hand and squeezed it. "We only want *one* dog, idiot!" she yelled back.

It wasn't until we'd knocked on the scratched front door and a young woman confronted us that there was any modification in the noise. She simply stepped past us, put cupped hands to her mouth and shrieked. That brought immediate silence. She turned and faced us.

"What do you want?" She was devoid of makeup, probably in her early twenties. I also noticed she was at least as pregnant as my friend. Jacqueline must have seen this just as quickly—and felt sisterly. At any rate, in reply to the lifeless voice from that wan and worried face, she replied brightly and with an easy warmth which I always found endearing.

She raised her hand to show a folded page from a newspaper. "We're so sorry to bother you but we read your ad in last Sunday's *Sun.* For Kerry Blues? You still have some unsold puppies, I hope? You had when I called last night."

The girl—for that is what she really was—wiped her forehead with the back of her hand. I noticed the bruised wrists and a similar discoloration at her temple. The notion of her as somehow prematurely broken by the harshness of life was compounded by my sense she was also a *victim.*

Once we'd followed her into the living room of the mobile home my thoughts about her were banished by the lurid environment. There were plastic mallards in brilliant turquoise nailed to the pink, stippled wall. The furniture suite to which she listlessly invited us, consisted of bright green armchairs with a companion sofa—all ornamented with a criss-cross gold thread. A shelf and sideboard, plus a glassed-in armoire, were crowded with cups and trophies from various dog shows. Crammed between bronze and silver statues were pennants and rosettes in blue and pink and yellow—announcing first, second and third class awards from canine competitions across western Canada and the United States. Further pennants adorned what little wall space remained and the minimal flat space that was left over was occupied with photos of dogs with handlers and judges, or just large portraits of Kerry Blues—some of them already faded with yellowing and mottled mats.

I was aware the young woman was eyeing me covertly. "My Dad showed Kerries," she said shyly. "I met my husband at a show and when we got married he brought his brood bitch, Irish Eyes, here to Dad's place. Dad had already bought Gahar's Choice of Kerry as our stud. All our stock traces back through Gahar. It's proper line-breeding, thanks to Dad."

I smiled encouragingly at her. Sitting opposite I thought her neck unusually red—as if hands had grabbed roughly there.

"It must be lonely here. You're a long way from the highway."

She wouldn't respond. Looked down at the stained nylon. A wall-eyed tabby sat curled in the remaining chair. That too, looked derelict as it wrapped a thin tail about its mangy body and stared hostilely back at me.

I wondered about the kennels and what condition the dogs might be in. Jacqueline read my thoughts. "Perhaps we could see the pups, then?"

The woman shrugged. "You can *see* 'em. You'll have to wait for Piet, though. He handles the business side. He should be back soon. He's gone to Langley to do a bit of wiring for Andreas Staedler. He won't like it—strangers at the place without him knowing."

She led us through a filthy kitchen out to the barn where the dogs were housed. The barking flared once more but quickly died down at another screech from her.

If the interior of the house depressed by its garishness, the barn lowered spirits in its damp gloom. For one thing, the small windows at the far end were so grimed and festooned with cobwebs the sun was just a tentative presence.

The dogs were housed in small runs in adjacent lines with a narrow corridor between those to the north and those to the south of the building. There were several single adults but Jacqueline and I were drawn to the sprawl of rotund little shapes, halfway down the center aisle. They were heaped in one corner. Keeping each other warm, I suspected, for the barn was chill and the puppy den had its stone floor scattered with soiled and chewed sheets of newspaper.

"That's their mother in the next pen," the woman informed us. "She's a swell brood bitch. Her milk's good and she keeps 'em real clean, eh?"

At the mention of motherhood and its concomitants I noticed the pregnant women glance at each other. Some sort of free-masonry at work, I decided. The girl smiled for the first time. "You got long to go?"

"About a month. And you?"

"They ain't sure. Early October, the first one told me. Then Piet changed my doctor 'cause he didn't trust him. The new one—he's much older, is Dr. Oliphant—he says not much before the end of the month."

Jacqueline reached over and grabbed a squirming pup; stroked its black, wavy coat. "Your first, I suppose?"

The Kerry Blue woman shook her head. "This'll be the third." She smiled—as if that were expected of her. "I had *twins* first, eh? They're with their Dad right now. He's real good. Takes them off my hands."

Jacqueline was obviously taken aback by the news of the twins. I had the impression she hankered for the sweeter bond of two women confronting the prospects of their first-born. She went into what Ken and I referred to as her 'Queen Mum' routine.

"Twins! How delightful! How old are they and what are their names?"

I turned my head away to conceal a grin. The dog breeder took her words very seriously. She had no reason to know that Jacqueline could swiftly switch from that gracious pose to the bluntness of a French fishwife—as she was wont to do with her husband.

"They're goin' on five. Their names is Jack and Jill. Like in the nursery rhyme?"

My friend responded immediately—though I had been praying she wouldn't. Showing off her knowledge of all those *Englishy* little things *diminished* her in my eyes. Perhaps I was jealous of the scope of her erudition—considering I had no comparable understanding of her French culture.

She wasn't content, of course, with a quoting of *Jack and Jill Went Up the Hill*—had to persevere right through *brown paper, vinegar* and *broken crowns* to the very last *tumbling after.* When she was finished there was a silence, except for the small yelps from the various puppies.

The younger woman simply stared at her. "That's nice," she said. "Fancy you remembering it all—you bein' a—"

She stopped. I knew she'd been about to add "a foreigner." Madame Murphy wasn't at all fazed. She quickly strove to rescue her sister-in-pregnancy from a social gaffe.

"Nursery rhymes were the first thing I learned in English!" she exclaimed gaily. "My mother made us all recite children's poems like 'The Noble Duke of York' and 'A Frog He Would A-Wooing Go.' "

"Really," said the woman dully—convincing me she'd never heard of either. "My husband's Dutch and he's got a real way with them languages, too."

"Are you from the Lower Mainland?" I asked her, wanting in on the small talk. As if to avoid my question she bent over the wall of the makeshift pen and extracted another puppy.

"This little bitch is real feisty," she commented. "Goin' to be typey, too." Standing erect again she stroked the mewing pup, carefully eyeing it as she replied to me.

"Dad worked in Port Alberni at the mill until he bought this place. That's where I grew up, you might say."

There was a noise back towards where we'd entered. The three of us turned to look at the burly figure of a man silhouetted against the sunlight at the open door.

"You'll be telling 'em your old man was a drunk, next. They don't wanna hear all dat crap, Edna. I'm supposin' they're here to buy a good Kerry pup. It's their pedigrees they'll be wanting—not yours!"

Edna let the little wriggling female slide through her fingers, back to the concrete floor. "That's the only bitch in this litter, "she muttered. "Piet will show you. He knows more about it than I do."

Heavy farm boots clomped in our direction. We saw that the owner of the guttural voice was a florid man with thin reddish hair. He stood over six foot tall.

He ignored us and addressed his wife. "Get indoors. I left the twins there. The little bastards'll be pulling the place apart!"

Edna started to move at once, slinking around his bulk—as if half-expecting a punch to help her on her way. Jacqueline bridled at this—or at the proprietary tone he'd used with his wife.

"We're here to *see* your pups—not necessarily to buy one. I've no means decided whether a Kerry Blue is the right breed for my husband and me."

He nodded insolently at her belly. "Be right enough for what you got in there. Kerrys is good with kids."

He turned to me. I forced my sight to meet his cold stare. I sensed my skin grow hot as he brazenly sized up my masculinity—and found it wanting. "Take care of your husband, too, would a Kerry. Damn good guard dogs."

She ignored both his reference to her condition and the fact he obviously mistook me for Neil.

"And just how gentle would one be with a tiny baby pulling its tail or tugging at its ears?"

"Best dogs in the world with kids—I already told you. If you don't believe me, why don't you ask my old lady about any dog here with her and the twins?"

"I hardly got the chance," Jacqueline said icily.

He ignored that. "She wouldn't be having another kid if she didn't think it okay with these dogs. She feeds the lot of 'em and cleans 'em all out."

"I can well imagine," Jacqueline said meaningfully.

He became defensive. "I got too much on my hands going to all them shows and getting their Canadian and American championships. Not one of these adults ain't got its championship—she tell you that?"

The dogs were strictly Jacqueline's affair. I was reluctant to interfere. But he was eyeing me again. Again I had the impression he was unmasking me contemptuously.

"How much are these pups, then?" I asked primly. "I presume the litter is registered with the CKC?"

"You presume right." (Only a sanguine fool would have called his rictus a smile!) "One's already spoke. The other three? Seventy-five each. That's giving 'em away! Both sire and dam have their championships—CKC *and* AKC. And the sire's gone Best of Breed and Best in Show at every show I've took him to."

Mercifully, Jacqueline took over again. He deliberately started scratching about his genitals. His overt sexuality put wings to my imagination as

I stood there, transfixed by the cock contours pushing against the much-washed denim. I imagined the smell of the detergent-impregnated fly. I sweated in the exertion of forcing myself to stay in the realm of respectable reality.

"They look lovely pups, I admit," I remotely heard Jacqueline tell the Dutchman. "But there are a couple of other kennels I should visit before the final decision."

"Not in B.C. or Washington, there isn't," he growled. "Them's the best Kerry Blues you're going to see."

"I had other breeds in mind, too. It isn't the kind of thing to be rushed. You end up with a doggy for a long time."

Piet sniffed loudly, obviously miffed at the lack of a deal. "Well, I'm not haggling with you over the price. There won't be one of these critters left by Saturday's paper!"

Looking wistful, she carefully placed her puppy back with its brothers and sister. "Don't bother to show us out. We'll just step back to the car. Thank your wife for so kindly showing us everything. Please give her our best wishes over the new baby."

He followed us from a few feet behind. "Take some advice from an expert, lady," he told our backs. "Decide on the goddamn breed before bothering people. All pups is cute—you just put the likes of us to a lotta bother. That woman of mine got plenty to do without foolin' around."

There was a roughness to his voice which made argument risky. I was relieved Jacqueline made no rejoinder but kept pace with my brisk trot until we'd reached the car. She reversed at great speed down the rutted track. Neither spoke until the forlorn farm was buried from sight by the screen of deciduous trees.

When Jacqueline did give forth she exploded with a fiery denunciation of male brutes who broke the spirit of their child-wives in lonely places and then raped them. (This was an era when the protestations of liberated women were still largely in the future. Then my friend was always a bit of a prophet.)

As much in the interest of stemming her flood as the cause of moderation I pointed out her accusations were largely conjecture; that although his manner was boorish and his wife downtrodden, we were entirely without evidence he really was a wife beater or a rapist.

Jacqueline's response to this attempt to put brakes on her wrath rather startled me. "Of course you'd defend the bastard. I wouldn't expect anything else of a man!"

I was quick to point out that there were many who'd withhold that appellation from me. But she'd have none of it.

"Now you're going back to that ridiculous argument you used coming here. You must stop using the gay business as an excuse all the time. It prevents any proper discussion. The point is he was a pig and if I were married to him—obscene thought!—I'd soon teach him how to treat women. If Neil behaved like that he'd have a frying pan smashed down on his head!"

The resemblance between the burly Dutchman and elfin Neil was so bizarre I laughed out loud. She picked up on that immediately. "What big joke have I cracked? Can we send it to *Punch* or *The New Yorker*?"

I thought quickly of Piet's scratching his balls, and of my sudden response. Then of her bulging tummy. Almost simultaneously I recalled a cameo from the week before, when I'd walked into our bedroom at the tail-end of one of our more bibulous parties—to find Neil sprawled over a chair in front of Reid Forrest, a handsome heart surgeon from New Zealand. Reid had had his zipper down and Neil was offering quite different curves from those now frontally owned by his spouse.

"It isn't a woman's joke," I said. And proceeded to withstand all her pleadings for illumination.

THREE

≈

In the event, the Murphys purchased an eight-week-old Irish setter, and Jacqueline's baby—born three weeks to the day after our canine expedition—proved to be a boy whom they named Ben. I agreed to be a godfather when Jacqueline called to formally ask whether I would perform that function. It wasn't long before I was to wish I'd said no.

I realized something was up when Ken suggested we go for a walk through the Endowment Lands. I'd driven to campus one Friday afternoon to collect him before going shopping for another of our dinner parties. We are both creatures of habit and the normal Friday routine demanded that we drive straight to the Safeway on Upper Tenth. The wooded terrain skirting the campus was not our regular area for walks.

Ken immediately picked up a twig and started to peel it as we trudged the leaf-strewn path. "Neil came into my office today for a long talk," he began. "He's quite pissed off with Jacqueline."

As usual, I bridled in her defense. "So what else is new?"

"He's upset because she's gone right ahead with arrangements for the christening without telling him. You know how he is."

"I most certainly do! A frustrated you-know-what who takes his repressions out on her." I couldn't see Ken's face as the narrow track determined he walk slightly ahead of me. But I was thoroughly familiar with the frown he'd be wearing whenever he was in disagreement with me.

"I said *how* he is, not *what* he is, Davey. In any case, I was talking about differences over religion—you know how they fight like cats when that comes up."

I did. Which is why I wasn't surprised when Ken elaborated on the incipient ruckus over the prospect of the infant Murphy's baptism into the Catholic Church. Neil was the kind of prickly atheist only a lapsed Catholic can possibly be. While Jacqueline, a Lyonnaise, possessed the stubborn persistence of the traditionalist French Catholic who, while scarcely darkening a church door through the average year, regarded Holy Baptism as a spiritual version of vaccination, marriage as only valid at the hands of a priest, and even burial as somehow botched if not processed through the ecclesiastical choreography of a requiem mass.

There had been heated arguments in the past when she'd insisted on attending Midnight Mass on Christmas Eve while Neil demanded they throw an energetically bibulous party the same evening. Then they had compromised by agreeing to alternate years for the party-giving. According to Kenneth's account, as we walked through those quiet woods, there was little hope of such a solution to the baptism of baby Ben.

"Frankly, Davey, I don't think you'd better be one of the godparents. It'll only lead to more trouble. Not just between them but with us, too."

I knew Ken was being sensible and had obviously done a lot of thinking over the matter. Yet I balked. There is a constituent I possess of which I am often ashamed. It has also proved excessively costly. I refer to an instant hostility towards placatory compromise or, as I'm more prone to describe it, *pusillanimous* compromise. There are times when I'm forced to cite 'luck' as the major cement of our vaunted relationship of nearly twenty years when our friends get too sentimentally sloppy over it. . . .

"Don't forget, Ken, I've promised her. I simply can't renege on that, can I?"

"Something has to give," he said finally. "It's not just the baptism. He started by ranting about religion but soon got on to manipulation. I pointed out she might just as easily say he wanted to manipulate her—only he switched his hearing aid off at that point."

"It's all so stupidly familiar. If they can only bury the hatchet until Ben gets a bit older they'll at least have him to share."

Ken agreed readily. "In which case we must stop them rocking the boat right now. The puppy might help, too. At least it's something else for them to have to think about beyond themselves."

"What about trying to get them to postpone the baptism for a while? Do you think she'd agree?" I asked.

"Maybe. If it was put in the right way. No problem for Neil," Ken added. "He'd just think it a delaying tactic and would still put his foot down when the time comes."

"Well, I'll work on Jacqueline if you'll work on him," I offered. "It's the only thing I don't like about having kids. They're too often the ones that get hurt." Then I couldn't help adding with a smirk: "That's hardly a problem for gay couples, is it?"

Ken finished off the debarking process of his twig as the path widened and I grew abreast of him. "No it isn't," he agreed. "But we have our own trials, don't we?"

I knew what he meant, all right! By some kind of osmosis he'd guessed what I'd been up to the previous day. That after encountering a young man from Prince Rupert I'd repaired in a haze of desire to his hotel room. Or how a few weeks earlier, I'd found myself on a trail in Stanley Park, with a slim Greek sailor from a freighter moored in the bay.

Indeed, why, in those pre-AIDS days, should I stop there? The list of louche adventures in which my sex had involved me were constant during those years—had been so uninterruptedly—throughout my time with Ken.

It certainly wasn't something of which I was proud, nor was it something we ever discussed if I could help it. It existed between us as an intractable lump which wouldn't go away. But as long as my encounters were casual, one-time, and committed away from the home, the matter tended to be left there. Unsatisfactory but seemingly inevitable. . . .

So not surprisingly, I quickly changed the subject and suggested I mention baptismal postponement when I went with Jacqueline and her baby to visit Helen Goddard the next day.

My intention was to bring the matter up as she drove across town to the West End and I clutched the swaddled infant. But I hadn't bargained on Ben's disposition that blustery morning. He howled incessantly until we drew up outside the Goddards' high-rise. I also thought I could detect an unpleasant odour emanating from my unchristened godson.

By the time we entered the elevator I was somewhat out of humour and we didn't chatter away as we normally did. Jacqueline busied herself making nonsense noises at her noisy infant—to my distinct embarrassment when we were joined for the first two floors by another couple.

Things didn't improve. Helen straightway went into such a high-pitched screaming fit about the delectability of the baby that I momentarily wondered what I'd found so congenial about her on the ferry trip. She all but ignored me after offering me instant coffee. It was far worse than the freemasonry of joint pregnancy I'd encountered with Jacqueline and the cowed dog breeder. I could have taken a degree of exclusion from their conversation as two females exercising their commonalty but not this being wholly shoved to the circumference.

No one was rude, exactly. In fact they'd periodically descend from some kind of motherly high and ask me if I wanted a fucking biscuit—before returning to an endless catechism in which Helen plied questions covering baby's sleeping hours, skin rash, diaper changing, frequency of diarrhea, the size of his weenie, and the regularity of his sessions at Jacqueline's breasts.

I could have answered that for Helen, as Jacqueline was prone to whip out her tit to feed the brat and embarrass me, at every possible moment.

They moved on to his weekly addition of ounces and inches. The only variant to all this—if variant it could be called—was when Helen volunteered obsolete data about young Derek and sadly recalled that three years had now passed. The implication was she would have dearly loved a refresher course via a second child.

There came my chance! "It doesn't look as if it will be the case, does it? Gordon was quite adamant on the point at my birthday party, remember?" My interjection at least gave the women pause.

"Gordon really hasn't a clue as to what he wants," his wife said finally. "That's his problem." She leaned over the sofa to smile once more upon the now mercifully slumbering Ben. "I guess that is part of his charm, too. The little boy bit? Anyway, he's forever changing his mind over small things like fatherhood."

The ladies had the baby sprawled out on his blanket on the sofa between them. I was sitting in an armchair opposite, wondering how exactly one twiddled thumbs.

I had a brain wave. "Can I hold him for a while, Jacqueline?" Both glanced up. I read surprise on their faces.

"Of course. Though don't blame me if he starts to howl again."

I crossed immediately to the baby. I was afraid that Helen would anticipate me and bundle Ben to herself. I think I'd have struck her if she'd interfered as I gently lifted him in my arms and cradled him there.

My usurping of roles broke their maternal trance. As I sat down on the sofa between them the women rose. Jacqueline said she had to visit the bathroom and Helen told us there was something she had to do in the kitchen connected with lunch.

Benjamin now smelled fresh and talcumy (thanks, admittedly, to their ministrations). Through the baby clothes I could feel the high heat of his infant body. When they had left me alone—and I'd looked to be quite sure such was the situation—I held him close to my chest. He wasn't asleep for one blue eye looked lazily up at me. On tiny lips formed a little spit bubble which grew and diminished with his breathing.

I didn't do anything brash—like exposing my chest by opening my shirt a couple more buttons and directing that rosebud mouth towards the sterile pimple of my breast. But I did let all that flow through the reel of my mind. Not for the first time did I ponder the utility of those fossilized nipples we men have inherited. And I did slip my left hand surreptitiously into my shirt and touch the small protuberance above my left rib. I even recalled that when I'd lain with the young man from Prince Rupert on his hotel bed it had been surprisingly stiff around there. Yet now, with that dear little mouth so close, it was limp and impervious. I willed it otherwise, but without success. I heard the flush of the toilet and quickly returned my hand to my side.

When I was rejoined by my women friends, Benjamin had again closed both eyes and was sleeping happily. For a moment I felt a surge of content. Then the self-consciousness fled back in me, and the sense of celebration was gone. I suspected the colour pink interfered with my normal complexion.

"Here," I said to Helen, abruptly handing him to her. "Why don't you bounce baby for a bit—now that Derek's too old for it."

She took him from me readily enough, but she made me pay for the remark about her son by referring to my prior request for a stint with Jacqueline's child. "Did you feel all sorts of odd things stirring?" she enquired wickedly, settling the baby down again against her more bosomy bulge. "Did you want to be a real Mum for a second or two?"

If it had been Jacqueline who'd asked me the question I'd have called her a cow and had done with it. But I didn't know Helen as well and, besides, she'd caught me off guard.

"I can think of more exciting roles," I retorted. "Some of them might lead to motherhood but they don't have to. And they're quite delightful in themselves."

I have no idea why Jacqueline decided to enter the fray. Perhaps we were all getting hungry. "I bet they'd involve one of your lovely black boys, Davey. By the way, my sister—the one that works for Air France?—has got some nice snaps for you she took in Haiti. They are photos of the studs along the beach. I must say they sound very much your cuppa."

It was difficult enough to make specific allusions to my penchant for black men in front of Ken. It was impossible before these two women, one of whom was still virtually a stranger.

I capitulated then and there. "Talking of a cuppa—is anyone going to offer me at least a sherry before lunch?"

Jacqueline repented a little. "I think you'd make a super mother," she informed me. "But then you know I think you'd make a super father, too."

That brought Helen back into the chit-chat. "I wish he'd give a few lessons to Gordon. He's now talking of having Derek take ballet lessons the moment he's five and he wants me to agree to him already taking piano—and the poor kid's never even seen a pair of skates!"

"Artistic father wants artistic son," Jacqueline commented. "If Neil starts wanting anything like that for this one here, it'll be over my dead body!"

I didn't like the drift the conversation was taking. It was one thing to identify with the mothers—quite another to be disloyal to their mates. "Before you fight over whether Benjamin shall be an opera star or another Nijinsky," I opined, "I suggest you at least hold off on the baptism until Neil's in a more rational frame of mind."

Before we left Helen's (and, incidentally, a delicious lunch of eggplant soup and chicken livers) I actually got Jacqueline to agree.

FOUR

≈

In retrospect the routine of the next few months appears blurred. I am sure there were dinner parties between our three families and I know that the baptism was delayed for several months. When it did take place it was in a United Church where no godparents were formally required—indeed, wanted!

I shudder to think of the amount of blood spilled before this compromise was reached but I must admit that both Neil and Jacqueline appeared relatively equitable—at least during the simple church service and, initially, at the reception at their place afterwards. Neil's mother was visiting from Dublin. She stayed home and prepared the food we were scheduled to devour after a requisite amount of champagne, or the Bushmill's Irish, which her son was pushing.

Not that her decision to remain in the kitchen had been informed purely by kindly motives. We'd no sooner trooped in the front door when she appeared, wiping red hands down her black dress.

"So that's all over, is it? 'Tis after being a farce if you asks me. And how's me little darlin'? Not worth crying over, that lot!"

Her remarks may have been cryptic but they were not lost on some of us—Catholics or Protestants. Her only son had no more time for her ruffled Catholic sensibilities than for the Protestant Induction Service he'd just stonily attended.

"For Christ's sake, shut up!" he told her savagely. "It was bad enough sitting through that crap without hearing your bog superstitions afterwards. God Almighty! I've fled halfway around the world to escape that kind of balls!"

"Can I give you a hand, Mum? Shall I bring the food into the living room? You were an angel doing all that by yourself. I'm terribly grateful, really I am." Jacqueline offered her squalling infant almost as a peace-offering to her mother-in-law.

Whether the old woman was thus mollified we had no time to discover for others were pushing in behind us. It was obvious as Mrs. Murphy eagerly reached out scrawny arms to receive her grandson that he alone was the important factor for her in the rapidly crowding room.

As the two women and child headed for the kitchen, Neil smacked hands and asked whether we wanted French piss or Irish elixir. It was not a large baptismal party. The Murphys had asked us, along with the Goddards and their little boy, and beyond that, only a family named Ince. That consisted of parents Freddy and Joan, and their three small children: Ned, Mary and Julie. Freddy was a junior executive with Macmillan Bloedel, the giant lumber company, and sang in the Bach Choir with Neil—which is how they'd met.

Ken and I hadn't met any of them before and when we'd all sat down I started by chatting to the younger Inces. They were attractive children, blond and blue-eyed and strongly reminiscent of the British Royal Family with a small Prince Charles and Princess Anne. The boy, who was the eldest, turned out to be somewhat older than Derek Goddard, while the girls (who did most of the talking) were a little younger than their brother. It was the smallest, Julie, who fired a stream of questions at me. Ned sat quietly between his sisters, smiling politely and always speaking up in clearly enunciated tones when addressed directly. I took at once to the youngster and wondered if it was perhaps because I could dimly see something of myself in him. But all three were fetching and it was quite obvious that Ken, sitting next to me, thought likewise. I had never thought of myself as any sort of conservative in my social attitudes, yet it was their aura of old-fashioned politeness which drew me to these three children. Not that they were lisping 'Sir' all the time or bowing their pretty little heads like nuns when authority gave voice. But they sat upright on their chairs, folded hands, smiled readily, and genuinely participated in the party.

It sounds silly as I now write it, but I had the impression they all wanted us to be at our ease. There was also a virtuous quality about them—a universe from priggery, I should add—that evoked for me the precise opposite of young Miles in *The Turn of the Screw* when enthralled by Quint's evil. Then as I say, I was quite in danger of losing my heart to the sober little boy whose eyes stared so trustingly into mine.

His parents were a different story. Joan Ince was an attractive woman: the only person of either gender under the Murphys' roof whom I would unhesitatingly have described as beautiful. But as she sipped her champagne and laughed, and we discovered she was the sole native-born Vancouverite among the adults, I discerned a cool quality which disconcerted me.

The fact she was the mother of three suggested her coldness had nothing to do with sexual frigidity—but when I made a vague reference to a particularly salacious issue of the student newspaper which had recently been the talk of the town, I felt her will firmly at work, guiding me away from the topic. Ditto when I alluded to the fact Ken and I lived together—a fact I was damned certain she'd already learned from the Murphys. Here again I was grimly conscious of an icy determination to keep conversation on an innocuous level which discountenanced the kind of nervous talk which the presence of my lover and I could so easily evoke.

Perversity needed no summoning. I spent the major part of that afternoon winning her over, making her laugh, and more importantly, persuading her she was both witty and sophisticated.

The husband Freddy, whom I learned came from Oakville, Ontario and was educated at Upper Canada College and at the University of Toronto, didn't reveal much more than those *Who's Who* bunch of facts. He tossed his wife several devoted looks—which I duly recorded—and fussed far more over their children than she did. He reprimanded them in whispers or with a stern look if they laughed raucously or competed with one another in answering those incessant questions from the adults. I could see where they got the old fashioned bit from—but somehow it seemed more congruous in them than in their father.

At what period I would have learned more about Neil's colleague in the Bach Choir (or even whether I would have ever learned much more) was rendered academic by one of those minor coincidences that we often dismiss as literary devices when in fact they litter our lives.

Just one week after that christening party for Benjamin Patrick Murphy, I bumped into Freddy Ince at the Vancouver airport and we flew down to Toronto together—he to a forestry conference and me to a committee of the Writers' Union of Canada.

We were scarcely airborne before he referred to Upper Canada

College again and I wondered if he had only mentioned it at the Murphys because of my interrogation or whether it was some kind of an obsession with him. However, this time the context of his bringing it up was quite different.

"I wasn't too happy there, myself, and would just as soon Ned not go. But Joan is so terribly keen." He grimaced. "She thinks if he doesn't turn out too bright it will still give him some kind of advantage."

I thought of that little boy who not only seemed quite smart but, I felt sure, wasn't yet beyond the first grade. "There's still plenty of time, isn't there?"

He seemed immune from my mild sarcasm. "Of course, there's St. George's, or Shawnigan Lake over on Vancouver Island. Do you know anything about them?"

I said I didn't—adding that my knowledge of Canadian educational facilities was generally abysmal. "I know just a smidgen about such prep schools as Kent and Groton—and only because back in 1960, when I lived in New York, several people I knew had gone to such places. Episcopalians, of course."

"Boarding schools," he ruminated, "I think there's something basically unhealthy about them no matter what my wife says. Did you, by the way, go to what you Brits call a public school and come across that kind of thing?"

I got his drift and set my jaw. I wasn't going to satisfy his prurience—either on the ground or at 35,000 feet.

"The school I attended was what we called a boys' day school," I informed him. "And although it was founded in 1535 and attracted a few middle-class scholarship boys, it was fed mainly by poor East Enders."

"Oh," he said. It was obviously not quite the information he'd been seeking. He paused for a while and glanced out of the window at the cretaceous clouds, piled in echo over the snow-covered Rockies. I took the occasion to take a book from my briefcase.

The action seemed to galvanize my friend in the next seat. "I had a nasty experience at school. I think it has affected me."

"Really?" I didn't open my novel.

"Could you imagine me committing murder?" he asked quietly.

That certainly made me give him a hard look. I thought of a mousey man I'd once met in the library stacks of Stanford University, back in 1953, who I was subsequently convinced was the assassin of President Kennedy. Was Freddy Ince yet to commit his major transgression and earn a black footnote in history? I sighed involuntarily, as I am much given to doing. Airplanes tend to stimulate notions of mortality and sitting next to this tense young father of three, I felt cynical, ancient, and sadly deprived of a family.

Stupid, of course! I suspected I was infinitely more shrewd than Freddy Ince, was roughly the same age, and owned to a domestic life which was at least as fulfilling and warm as his.

"I have only once ever imagined I was in the presence of a murderer —and that entirely without substantiation. But if you are about to play airplane confessions, Freddy, I should warn you I am no priest. I flee from other people's complications whenever I can. I believe it is called selfishness."

I think all that rather overwhelmed him. Anyway, he back-tracked at a conspicuous rate. "Of course, I've never done anything *really* violent, let alone murder. It's only that I was once terribly upset, as I said. I think it's turned me into a prude." He smiled wanly in my direction. "I have to tell you that because it was a bit on my conscience when we were at the Murphys'."

I said nothing. I had decided long before that I wouldn't help people conversationally from trouble of their own making, if it were at all connected with my relationship with Ken.

He audibly gulped for breath. "Professor Ken Bradley has known Neil Murphy for a long time? I gather they're great friends on campus but Dr. Bradley isn't in English with Neil, is he?"

"Ken teaches French. He and Neil started at UBC around the same time. I guess that would be two—no, three years ago."

"It was a nice service, wasn't it? Though I gather Neil doesn't take too much to that kind of thing. I understand you're a good friend of Jacqueline's?"

I signaled to the stewardess to stop with her wagon of drinks and ordered a vodka and tonic. Then I turned once more to my companion. "Ken and I are very good friends of the Murphys. Either—they left it to us—could've been a godfather had Benjamin ended up being baptized in the Catholic Church."

Freddy refused a drink when asked. "Old Mrs. Murphy is a charmer, isn't she?" By which I inferred that Freddy Ince had concluded his ferreting over my and Ken's curiously unmarried existence. Or rather that he'd gone as far as his boldness would allow.

Only now it was I who was reluctant to let matters slip back into neutrality. "You still haven't told me about what happened to you at school. I want to know more about that nasty experience you referred to." I have to confess to a smidgen of pleasure at the grimace my request evoked.

"It was my housemaster," he said quickly, "He—he made an improper suggestion. It was quite horrible."

"You mean he wanted you to snitch on another boy?"

Poor Freddy's face was now close to crimson and if he didn't exactly lose his voice it went incredibly low. "Nothing like that, I'm afraid. The man was—well, he wanted me to be his *catamite.*"

Even I, instinct with mischief and malice whenever confronted with prudery, had not the cruelty to demand excessive elaboration. Yet I was incapable of leaving it just there. "What, may I ask, is a catamite?"

The ensuing pause wasn't merely pregnant: it was more like a protracted birth. "A—a *bum*-boy," Freddy shuddered.

I relented. "Is that now the most vivid memory of your school days? Weren't there perhaps more pleasant things, too?"

"I never finished at Upper Canada College. My father died. We were suddenly much poorer. I dropped out. But I won't bore you with all that." He stared fixedly at the net pocket of the seat in front of him, at part of the cover of the airline's magazine.

"I suppose having children, especially a son, you've always got schools and educational costs on your mind. There at the Murphys' it wasn't only our own boy, but the Goddards' Derek, who's not that much younger. And then, of course, the Murphy baby. When we got home Joan reminded me of the three boys and started on the UCC thing again for Ned. I think

I just associated you with the occasion at the Murphys' and when we met on this flight, it all came flooding back."

You're a bloody liar, I said to myself. But my reluctance to embark upon a conversation centering on catamites with this tongue-tied mass of confusion helped me to refrain from stating I thought it was my bachelor presence which had sparked the recollection of Freddy Ince's *Bum-Boy Schooldays.*

It was not difficult to get him onto less onerous topics. With only minor prompting he embarked on those friends we shared in common—the Murphys, and, in more superficial vein, the Goddards.

Not that it was solely my skillful prodding and Freddy's passive response. In fact he rather took me aback when he suddenly asked whether I believed baby Benjamin was the result of a lovers' reconciliation after a quarrel.

"Did some of your kids arrive that way, then?" I asked brightly. Freddy was agreeably shocked—and I was able to warm to him once more.

If I sound cynical it's because I'm persuaded it is only poor Freddy's shockability which has been the bond between us down through the years since that plane ride. After all, I love shocking—and when you have a perfect patsy it's a kind of power relationship which emerges. In this case with me on top.

He, of course, I'm sure saw it quite differently. His ability to be readily aghast he actually saw as moral strength. His reluctant acceptance of the situation between Ken and me has subsequently persuaded him of his charitable liberalism—of which he is inordinately proud. So, like all successful relationships say I, still playing the cynic, it is *symbiotic:* a mutually beneficial arrangement.

We had passed over Winnipeg when we were subject to one of those profound silences which happen on journeys after an initial burst of conversation. I had, in fact, returned to my book when Freddy took up the threads of talk again. Only the subject was wholly other.

"What made you decide to come to Vancouver to live?"

I have two standard answers to that question—neither of which is strictly accurate. The first suggests I visited from California, enjoyed what I saw, and elected to stay. The second—tied more closely to the truth—is that Ken and I liked what we saw and that, once it was established he could teach at the University of British Columbia and I could earn an adequate income from free-lancing, the choice of Vancouver was a natural one.

Both Ken as a Californian, and I as a Cornishman, were born to see the sun setting on oceans. We were also jointly put off by the notion of humid eastern and midwest summers and had no experience (nor wanted any) of severe winters. Given these factors our response to coastal British Columbia was well nigh inevitable. The first explanation was usually accorded those who knew nothing of our relationship and whom I wasn't prepared to enlighten. The second rationale was for those familiar with my gay background and who'd not make heavy weather over such knowledge.

Problem: which category to allot Freddy?

"I visited the northwest when I was doing a travel story for my San Francisco editor," I began, then decided to bring at least a bit of 'answer number two' into the explanation. "And by sheer coincidence," (a lie) "Ken was offered a job in the French Department at UBC."

"I've often wondered about those travel stories," Freddy replied. "Are you free to say what you want or do you always have to be positive?"

I anticipated then, with dull certainty, the safe rails on which our relationship would be running—from its dawn there in the cloudless prairie skies, to the dusk of our future. It is that which ensured the perpetuation of an acquaintanceship rather than a friendship, even if at a distant date, there should be a peculiar rubbing together of family destinies. But of that odd confluence, more later. . . .

FIVE

≈

It should never be said that my friendship with Helen Goddard was to appear calmly balanced over time. From the outset there were little spurts of—what? Antagonism? Jealousy? Just sheer competitiveness?

Some of the skirmishes were no more than puerile. A game of Scrabble with Americanized me supplying sox as a plural and Helen insisting on the exclusive legitimacy of socks.

There were more signal oppositions. Several of these occurred when for the first time we five took a vacation together. We were thus bereft of those useful rat-runs of our daily lives when each knows when to push and when to desist; when to dodge and when to retreat. This proved one of those occasions when all the skills honed in domesticity are no longer there to head off social abrasion.

Of course we were all younger then, back in 1968. The will to score, to prevail, was considerably more marked. I am not being entirely fair. I am referring to two particularly competitive types in Helen and me. *Leos*, Helen invariably called us, for she herself was a horoscope enthusiast from that period when such loomed ludicrously significant to many.

Up to that time we had only made shortish jaunts together but those had never encompassed more than a weekend and with Derek still dependent enough to absorb much of his mother's febrile energy.

Now, though, we were to take the slow route along the Mendocino Coast to San Francisco and then, if time allowed, on further south to Monterey, Carmel, and perhaps to the Big Sur which was familiar and cherished terrain for Ken and me.

We stopped the first evening within driving distance of the famous Sea Lion Caves on the Oregon Coast. Ken and I were quite pooped as we had attended a party the night before in Vancouver and the chauffeuring was entirely ours as at that time neither Gordon nor Helen drove.

At the approach to the caves there occurred a typical friction between Helen and me. Nothing dramatic. More like lazy lightning heralding a summer storm. Derek, not unnaturally, was dying to descend the myriad steps to see the sea lions. Helen and Gordon, as properly fond parents, were anxious to accommodate him. But my own instincts—and Ken tends to follow suit—is to avoid tourist spots on principle. Thus we've never ascended the Eiffel Tower, climbed the Empire State Building or the Statue of Liberty, or lingered at Stonehenge, Pisa, or San Francisco's Fisherman's Wharf. The latter was to prove particularly germane to this account but only after the *contretemps* surrounding the Sea Lion Caves and Fort Ross along the Mendocino Coast.

First there came Derek's request to his parents, followed by Helen's announcement of the itinerary which had to be taken through the Caves. I accepted the Goddards' demands, of course, which I thought quite reasonable on the face of it. It was only their presentation which sparked the resentment which erupted the following day when it came my turn to suggest we spend time at Fort Ross.

The Russian fort, with its wooden stockade stuck out on a rather desolate sweep of coastline and the minuscule Orthodox church huddled within one corner of it, has a sentimental place in my heart. Ken and I lived with White Russians in Paris when we first met and the Russian Liturgy was substantive in our young lives.

That wasn't the exclusive reason why I announced, with comparable stridency to that which Helen had invoked over the Oregon caves, that we were stopping at Fort Ross for some time. There was no immediate rebellion, or even hesitation, on the part of our three passengers. Young Derek, indeed, seemed more enthusiastic than he had over the bloody sea lions twenty-four hours earlier. Even Gordon (who always seemed somehow out of place in the open air) expressed curiosity in the nineteenth century fur-trading bastion. Until, that is, we actually arrived at the onion-domed church.

"This is a bunch of nonsense," Helen announced. "There's nothing original. It says in this leaflet the whole lot's been burned down. Not just once either!"

"We *know* that, dear," I said patiently. "But the reconstruction's been fairly authentic, even if the wood smells and looks new."

"I hate fake things," she persisted, squeezing past us into the open stockade again. Gordon looked distinctly unhappy and mumbled something about Tudor architecture—an amateur enthusiasm of his.

His small son tugged at my arm. "Is this where they had all their funerals, Uncle Davey?" He was a child with a decidedly morbid cast of mind I'd often observed.

"I doubt it," I told him. "They weren't here all that long and just bought sea otter furs in the name of the Czar and sailed back across the Bering Straits to Siberia."

Derek looked unconvinced. "I thought churches was for weddings and for funerals."

"Lots are. But this was more like a chapel. The Orthodox priest would accompany the traders. They were very devout people."

"When they weren't bashing in the heads of sea otters," said Gordon.

I bridled immediately at the gentler of the two adult Goddards. "Considering your enthusiasm for history, it's not very historical to allot 20th-century sentiments to 19th-century attitudes over hunting otters, whales or seals." Which he hadn't done, of course.

It was hard to rile the compliant Gordon. "Oh, I agree! Certainly the Russians were no worse than the British or Americans in their slaughtering. It was a stupid remark."

His placatory words didn't help at all. They heaped further coals on his wife for leaving the church precipitately.

"I want to take a closer look at some of these icons," I announced to Gordon and Ken. "In spite of Helen's response I rather think they're authentic. Even ancient."

The two drifted off but the kid elected to stay with me. "Why is that picture so dark, Uncle Davey?" Derek asked. "Is that a Negro lady?"

We were standing by an icon of Our Lady of Kiev, which I could now see was a modern version—and amateurishly executed at that. I suspected they all were, in spite of my prior statement.

"They are dark because of the varnish used on them," I explained. "And when they're in churches they probably get darker and darker because they often have smoky candles burning before them."

"What'd they have candles for?" Derek asked instantly. But I wasn't in the mood to answer a stream of penetrating questions from an intelligent eight-year-old.

"Let's join your father and Ken," I suggested. But if the child was prepared to forego an interrogation on the meaning and use of icons, he was not content to supinely follow my bidding. Perhaps his mother was already making her genes felt in his developing character.

"You cross with Mummy?" he asked—abruptly enough for me to be taken off guard and actually blush.

"Me? Certainly not! Whatever put such a silly idea in your head?" I even patted it to demonstrate how warm and loving I felt. That he wasn't convinced I sensed from his next words.

"You didn't want to go down to the sea lion caves, did you Uncle Davey?"

"Well I didn't, did I? I'd been down there tons of times before. That's why I stayed in the car."

"Uncle Ken came down."

"Uncle Ken just adores sea lions. There's no holding him back when they're around!" He looked up suspiciously. He may not have understood sarcasm but he knew it was something he didn't like.

"Why?" I asked craftily. "Did Mummy say something about my staying on top?"

Unlike in me, there was no guile in little Derek. He frowned heavily in the task of recollection. "Mummy said . . . Mummy said you ate something and . . . and . . . "

"It hadn't agreed with me?" I supplied.

The boy's face beamed in recognition. Then he was anxious to yield more from his uncertain memory. "Mummy said you'd get over it. Yes, that's what Mummy said!"

I was tempted then and there to turn back and spend a week at least, examining the ancient icons of Fort Ross. Proportion finally came to the rescue. "Let's go and see if Mummy's feeling well, shall we? I don't think being in this little church agreed with her very much, either."

Outside in the sunlight, in the liberation of ocean skies, and in the approach of another small knot of tourists inspecting the fortifications, my mood relaxed. I was relieved young Derek abandoned the subject of his mother and myself. Instead he cartwheeled on the bumpy turf and then sidled up to Helen, who was standing with arms folded looking out over the Pacific. Her son wondered aloud if it were not warm enough for an ice cream.

Helen turned from the ocean to me. "Why don't you ask Uncle Davey about lunch," she said. "Then you could have ice cream as dessert."

I suggested we eat right away (as solution to several impasses). After deluxe hamburgers and delicious fries, we were all again in high spirits as we sped the snaking cliff road southward to San Francisco.

The next couple of days were crammed with sight-seeing on the part of Ken, Gordon and young Derek, while I dutifully escorted Helen amid the counters of the City of Paris, the White House and the Emporium, followed by detailed inspection of more retail establishments such as Gump's and Brooks Brothers.

Helen, an indefatigable shopper, was in her element and although my feet ached with trudging and my eyes blurred with the prodigious examination of uncongenial objects, I did vicariously participate in her delight and gladly helped her with the numerous goods destined to be smuggled back into Canada.

It was only when the shopping spree was over and Ken and Derek had exhausted the tourist sites that we reunited for our last day in the city.

At breakfast near the motel Helen suggested a visit to Fisherman's Wharf as our final expedition. Sea lion caves and images of dreary department store lunch floors rose rebelliously in my mind.

"Fisherman's Wharf, dear, is a ghastly tourist trap. Why don't we take a drive across the Presidio, cross the Golden Gate again to Tiburon? We could have lunch at an old place called the Alta Mira above Sausalito. Ken and I love having lunch there. The view towards Alcatraz is marvelous."

My suggestion brought silence around the table. Ken broke it, treacherously, I thought. "Maybe Sam's at Tiburon would be better. I'm sure Derek would love the hamburgers and the ice cream dishes are special, too."

Bugger little Derek for once! Is the whole bloody trip supposed to be built around him? (But they were merely unspoken thoughts in my head.) More silence ensued. I was a little surprised when Gordon, not Helen, broke it.

"Derek's just learning baseball at school, aren't you, pet? You know, Joe di Maggio was one of the most famous ball players in the world, don't you? His restaurant is on Fisherman's Wharf." He smiled at his tousle-haired son. "Good food would be wasted on him, Davey. But on balance," he added judiciously, "I vote we take Ken's hamburger place in Tiburon. Sausalito sounds fun, too. We pass through it on the way, don't we?"

I thought it quite clear he and Ken had already had detailed conversation about Marin County. I wondered crossly why they hadn't brought up the suggestion themselves—rather than let Helen plumb for Fisherman's Wharf and me for the Alta Mira.

She and I exchanged glances. I think we decided simultaneously it was a stand-off. "I wouldn't want to pander to tourist traps," she said with a ghost of a smile. "Besides, I've had a smashing shop for two whole days."

It was my turn to be gracious. "We can eat at a really swank restaurant in Carmel. And the Fisherman's Wharf in Monterey is much nicer than this one, isn't it, Ken?"

But Ken was already fooling with Derek—playing some idiot guessing game. I resolved that in the quiet of bed time I'd have a little chat with my roommate about co-operation and loyalty. In the meantime it was apparent Tiburon and Sam's had gotten the vote.

With all the tension clouds evaporated we headed for the eucalyptus shade of the Presidio and after watching humming birds far below the Golden Gate Bridge, passed time at a bookstore in Sausalito before continuing on to the Tiburon dock.

Next day was the open road once more to Monterey Bay. It was there an incident occurred which was illuminating of the most covert of our party. After brimming cocktails before a superfluous fire in Carmel's Pine Inn, we dined at the small French restaurant I'd mentioned to Helen. Derek left half his underdone steak and all his over-seasoned vegetables. We grown-ups relished the meal, though, and, in blithe mood, returned to our motel where Derek went straight to bed, Ken and Helen prepared to watch television (and the sleeping boy) while Gordon and I left ostensibly for a walk amid the magenta mysthembreanthemum of the shoreline. We actually drove to the more raunchy environs of Old Monterey in search of a little nightlife.

We parked the car near the adobe Customs House and found ourselves at the open entrance of a long bar—the backdoor of which was also open and affording a glimpse of a charcoal sea and star-pricked sky.

A discreet sign proclaimed the water-hole as the Golden Fleece and from the interior a jukebox box played some current Broadway hit. It wasn't just the plethora of men in white, tight-fitting pants standing at the bar which proclaimed this a gay establishment. With a quick exchange of glances, we sauntered in. Gordon ordered us gin-and-tonics and several heads turned quickly at the sound of his British accent.

Sitting on an adjacent stool was a youth in the uniform white pants and a striped sailor's T-shirt. In spite of the severely dimmed light I could see his blond curls had been given a helping hand by other than the sun.

He smiled prettily and addressed Gordon. "Hi. You guys from the Army Language School?" Less like an army or a language I had never felt and was about to say so when Gordon forestalled me.

"We're from Vancouver, Canada," he announced. "This is our first visit to California." He corrected himself. "It's *my* first visit. My friend used to live in San Francisco."

Ken has taught me to dislike it when people give away too much information about themselves—especially right off the bat. I decided to help out. "It's the first time, though, I've ever been here," I told the young man in the suggestively tight pants. "Has the Golden Fleece existed very long?"

"Ages! Hey, José!" He called the jet-haired bartender over. "How long this place been here, Mother?"

José had our drinks in his bejeweled hands. "Let's see, I've been working here for six years and I'm twenty-five."

The black hair didn't start until way back on his sun-tanned head.

Besides, there were tell-tale wrinkles about his neck and under his eyes. I gave him a good ten years more than his admission. Fortunately no one took him up on it. We didn't have to listen to a lot of tired old reparteé.

"Funny I've missed it," I said. "Been down on the Peninsula several times."

"You probably know the Schooner," José volunteered. "On the wharf? It's more lively than this *dump.*" He gave the correct Bette Davis inflection, and I felt a twinge of boredom.

Gordon travelled different rails. He looked at our bartender, at the friendly neighbour perched on the bar stool and smiled. "It seems very nice here," he said warmly. "I wouldn't call it a dump."

I could've hugged him for his innocence. "Gordon doesn't know Bette's movies like the rest of us. He's a married man. More than that—he's the daddy of one smart little boy."

As I expected, that caused more patrons to turn in our direction. Lots of gays love young daddies. What I was *not* expecting was Gordon's reaction to my disclosure. He simply stared at me—in what seemed like an anguish of disbelief.

"Don't!" he shrieked. "You've no right to tell them! I don't—these primping *faggots* mustn't know!"

It struck me with overwhelming force just how desperate he was for social concealment as a gay. I realized anew that if he hated his sexual peers in the bar he hated himself more. I sighed. "I'm sorry, Gordon. That was stupid. I shouldn't—"

He didn't wait for more—just fled the way we'd entered. I was delayed, searching for the money to pay, before hurrying after him.

Outside, away from the bar and the lights beyond, the streets of Monterey were dark and deserted. My feet echoed noisily as I ran down one after another in pursuit of my friend. I had the feeling he'd avoid both light *and* people, so made my way steadily up the slopes leading away from the water's edge.

When I eventually came across him it was in a small park bordered by palm trees and containing an ornamental lake. I thought I could see the outline of the Mission building in the distance.

Gordon was standing at the base of a tall eucalyptus which filled the night air with its fragrance. I could tell him by his silhouette. His shoulders were jerking. He was crying. "Go away!" he said brokenly.

I ignored him and put my arm about his shoulder. He didn't resist. To the contrary, I felt him snuggle closer. I realized my proximity was providing some measure of comfort—at least compensating for my behaviour in the Golden Fleece.

As the sobs subsided he slowly found voice. "Sorry about that. I don't usually come apart at the seams. It's only I suppose I live two different lives. I couldn't live any other way. It's bad enough to have *her* suspicions. But for Derek to know—well that's just unthinkable. I'd kill myself before letting him find out!"

His words made me unutterably sad. "Do you want to go home?" I asked gently, meaning the motel. He misunderstood me—perhaps deliberately.

"*All* of me can never go home," he said wistfully. "There's always a part out here in the dark, wandering through the parks."

I recalled our conversation when I'd first known him and he'd enquired about steambaths. "There were the tubs," I said. "The steamers you asked about. I thought you were going regularly to them by now, I don't know why."

"I did for a while," he admitted. "Then I saw Neil Murphy one night. I had to duck out the back way. I don't think he saw me."

"Would it have mattered all that much?"

He shrugged. "To me it would. But that just put an end to Dino's. I still went on visiting the Richards Street Service Club. But in the end that proved even worse. I saw someone from my office at B.C. Tel."

I fell back on an old point of reassurance for nervous closet types. "If he saw you, then you saw him. The thing's mutual, you know."

He shook his head, unconvinced. "That's not the way I want it."

I was tempted to tell him he was just being obstinate. That there was far less danger of discovery in a steambath than out there in the park. But I held myself in check. After all, I wasn't a father—knew nothing of such strains and fears. I wasn't a husband either.

"Are you absolutely sure Helen doesn't know? That's not the way she seems to me. God knows, she talks about it enough!"

"She suspects, of course. But there's a hell of a gap between suspicion and certainty. Every married gay knows that, I can tell you!"

There was something about what he said which intrigued me. "How could you possibly know? Is there some special club for gay men with wives and kids?"

He smiled grudgingly. Not for the first time I thought how attractive he was. Forbidden fruit syndrome, probably.

"Sort of. Take Saturday afternoons. We're all out with the wives shopping. We leave 'em among the fabrics or appliances and head to the johns for a 'quickie.' There's hardly ever time for real sex. Just a grope and feel. Maybe a kiss. The rest is stored up in memory for a time on one's own when you can remember his tool and his face and play with yourself and think of what might've been."

His voice was as desolate as his words. I sighed. "Perhaps one day you'll be able to tell her."

He looked me in the eye. "Perhaps. But when that happens everything really important will be over between us."

We got back to find Ken and Helen still watching an installment of *Ironside* on TV while Derek slept soundly on the camper bed provided.

We stayed, had a nightcap of the scotch we carried with us before returning next door. I informed Ken of the events of the evening. He listened in silence until I was through before reaching over and pulling the light cord. For a moment we lay silent in the dark.

"Not a word of this to Helen, Davey. You've got to be very careful."

I was discountenanced by his tone. "But he told her as soon as we got in that we'd been to a bar."

"He neglected to say it was a gay one."

"What kind of bar do you think she believes you and I go to?"

"That's not the point. Anything he tells her is fair enough. But she can be difficult. We musn't get too involved in their problems. It won't help either."

"Couldn't agree more. But what am I supposed to say if she asks me outright? Lie?"

"Tell her to ask her husband. Tell her you must be loyal. Take the Fifth! Do what you like, sweetheart. You will, anyway!"

I had been through one emotional upheaval that evening. I didn't want another with my lover. "Goodnight," I said gently.

He returned the salutation with even more tenderness.

The subject of gay bars did come up with Helen—the very next day. Her approach to the subject, though, was more circumspect than usual. We had bought food for an outdoor picnic and were sitting at Point Lobos State Park, staring out at a lagoon which was as aquamarine as anything in Capri.

I was feeling drowsy as we idly watched sea otters play amid the kelp while Derek caught grasshoppers when they jumped onto the tartan rug, his father supervising to see he wasn't dismembering them. The rest of us, I suspected, gazing down the slope of the bleached cliffside, were prisoners of our introspection.

I know my own thoughts had winged their way back to a roughly comparable cove to this one in the Cornwall of my childhood. Ken was wearing what I called his Huntington Library look which involved a dreamy middle-distance gaze and slightly parted lips, inferring a special content. The Huntington Library in Pasadena and this state park were two of his favourite places.

Suddenly Helen said to me: "When we start back, after Big Sur and all that, will we be going through Monterey again?"

I grinned, thinking she was alluding delicately to a further bout of shopping. "There's not too much room left in the trunk," I told her. "But I guess we could squeeze things in if you found what you wanted."

She wiggled a bare toe impatiently. "Dumb-dumb! I wasn't thinking about anything of the kind. You're as bad as Gordon—trying to second-guess me."

"Forgive my rude impetuosity," I said. "What did your ladyship have in mind? A game of golf at Pebble Beach?"

"A drink at the bar you and Gordon went to last night," she announced flatly.

"I don't want to go back there," her husband said quietly, still playing with his son. "You three can go."

"Okay, if you don't like that bar, we'll go to another one," Helen persisted. "Let Ken and Davey decide. I'd just like to go to a place where the two of you would go if you were on your own. There's probably somewhere you prefer."

"I see. You want to see how the other ten per cent live," I joked.

"Davey and I aren't really bar-flies," Ken said, sounding uncomfortable. "We like to talk too much and most of the gay bars—I presume that's what we're speaking about—are all noise and darkness."

"I don't care," Helen insisted. "Until I experience all that noise and all that darkness, I'll feel my education's been neglected."

"Not all knowledge is necessary," her husband pedantically observed. He was even-toned but I sensed his reproof.

So could she. "Do you mind?" she said icily. "As you've dropped out of the picture at your own request, I'm talking to my *friends.* At least I know they'll be honest in saying what they feel. That's more than could be said for some around here."

The cut of that, the sheer loathing, made me wonder. It reminded me, oddly, of the private mystery of one's friends' finances. But I would rather have discussed the Goddards' income and its disbursement than become entangled in the hate which suddenly ran like fire about their words.

"I'm an honest boy, Mummy! Aren't I, Dad?"

I never loved little Derek more on the whole trip than at that moment. "Of course you are," she told him. "It wasn't you I was thinking of, darling."

But the child wasn't disposed to follow that one up. "Can I have a vanilla ice cream, then? For being honest?"

"You must wait a little bit, Derek," I told him. "There's no ice cream man out here. But if Mummy agrees I'll get us all to a Dairy Queen later this afternoon."

"You don't have to treat him, Davey," Gordon said. "Let them all be on me."

"That son of mine is getting to *look* like an ice cream cone," his mother grumped. But at least her words weren't a direct attack on her husband.

with his father's delicate eyebrows above long lashes, and his mother's quick mouth to express the vivacity he'd inherited from her. He wasn't tall but he had a poise to his walk which somehow conferred on him an exotic quality, separating him from his coevals.

Apart from the fact I'd been as blond as Benjamin was dark, I couldn't refrain from comparing him to myself at the same age as we left the fresh verge of the boulevard and entered the cool of the reborn deciduous forest. He was indubitably more talky!

As we penetrated further and further into the emerald gloom, the path grew narrower and its surface more squelchy. We soon had to walk Indian file. Not that that bothered Benjamin, who vocally percolated as steadily as ever! Although his chatter included an enormous number of questions he hardly seemed to need my presence to answer them.

"You know, Davey, I could ride my bike through here, couldn't I? I would have to stay out of the mud, though. I bet a whole lot of mud could swallow you up. Have you ever been swallowed up by mud, Uncle Davey?"

"No, but mud once saved my life." That shut him up, just as I'd hoped it would. Or nearly did. He had just one more question. "What—what happened over there in—in—" I knew he was trying to remember Cornwall and I was flattered.

"In Cornwall? My uncle's granite quarry? My cousin Jan and I . . . It was a Sunday afternoon so it was deserted. We found this little tip-up car on the track that ran from the cliff-face to the crusher, way over the moor."

"What's a crusher?"

"Shut up and let me go on—right?" Silence. "We pulled the car further and further up the slope. We both sweated a lot I remember. The rails were rusty and there was bracken—that's a little like those ferns in front of you—covering the tracks. In the end we were having longer and longer rides each time.

"The last time I could see we were going to smash right into the crusher. It headed closer and closer. Then, all of a sudden, an invisible brake took over. Just as I hit some corrugated metal I managed to look down. It was mud which had slowed us. I passed out. I'd cracked a couple of ribs but the mud saved my life."

"Could we drown in this mud, Uncle Davey?"

"No," I said. "This is a different kind of mud. It wouldn't save your life either. The stuff on that moor is what bogs are made of. Men on horseback, Benjamin, have sunk in it and never been seen again."

Soon after that I pointed out a Cooper's hawk to him in a grassy clearing we reached. Then, by some marshy ground, a few yards on, a red-winged blackbird clung precariously to a dried bullrush. It was at that point I told Benjamin we had to stop talking altogether if we were not to frighten all the wildlife away.

The trail came out eventually at a beach area of scattered boulders and numbers of surf-feathered tree-trunks.

Even Sean was having to struggle more and more over the terrain and we had not gone far before I pantingly suggested we stop for a breather.

When we started up again, I was just a little ahead of my godson, as we continuously climbed over logs and rocks. Then abruptly, right ahead, I saw the recumbent figures of a naked couple side by side in the lee of a log. I called myself several kinds of fool in taking that particular route—for I wasn't wholly ignorant of either the frequent nudity or what else transpired in those remote reaches of the city's shoreline.

I told Benjamin to make no sound but to closely follow me as I began to ascend the steepest boulder—where the alder and brambles grew most thickly. Whether our species still responds to ancient urges in the springtime I am unsure, but certainly that late morning, in the company of my ten-year-old charge, I received the distinct impression that the whole human race was in rut!

The man and woman we had left below may, or may not, have shed garments for the sole sake of receiving the sun's blandishments. There was no way that could be the interpretation of the ensuing tableau of a couple, locked in writhing embrace; conjoined at mouth and crotch as he pushed her for support against the bole of an innocent birch.

Benjamin, who by now was at my side, offered me a look which had nothing to do with the artlessness I was inclined to associate with small boys. But my shock at his impish grin was diverted by the sight of an insouciant Sean, wandering towards the lovers and their tree, with a gait which made me think he might cock his leg over them.

There was no stage whisper about my next action. "Sean!" I yelled. "Heel!" The aging setter looked mildly surprised but immediately did as he was bid.

It was the same moment the pumping between the young couple jerked to a halt. I hope he didn't bite her tongue off but I have seldom seen a male jaw clamp tighter and more swiftly. And I speak from considerable experience.

In self-conscious silence we proceeded past them—with Master Murphy flinging arms rhythmically before him as he goose-stepped like a Wehrmacht soldier. I sagged with relief when my lad finally led us safely out of sight and earshot.

That was not to prove the end of tense or torrid moments on that day. About a half-hour later, when we'd described a wide curve, and were back within sound of the sea below, we came across a single man wearing an unnecessary raincoat as he skulked about the tall clumps of yellow broom that separated us from the edge of the cliff.

By now I was prepared for anything—or so I thought. If he proved a child-molester I'd leap in defense of my spiritual progeny; if a murderer with a corpse hidden somewhere amid the broom, I'd make a citizen's arrest. And if just a Peeping Tom, then I would shame him into fleeing with coarse catcalls.

Unhappily, he proved to be none of these things. Ignoring Benjamin and Sean, the stranger made it obvious who he was interested in. He never came right up to me but from the moment that Ben (with a forceful shove from me) turned leftward, away from him, the man was always in sight.

Whenever I turned to check if we'd eluded him—and he was fully viewable—his hand would descend below his waist and linger there. . . . The horrible thing was, I knew damn well if I'd been there alone I wouldn't be fleeing this well-built stranger.

"We always seem to be climbing the steepest parts," Benjamin suddenly grumbled. I flinched. I'd momentarily forgotten his presence.

"Sorry, Kid," I muttered, "I'm finding it a bit hard going myself." I wasn't exaggerating. I was not in particularly good condition. When we'd left the automobile it was with the intention of taking a leisurely nature walk—not a rehearsal for an assault on Mount Everest! Even in the shade of larch and cedars I sweated and every now and then had a nudge of vertigo.

I couldn't see the man behind us, now that trees and bushes were considerably more coniferous. But I thought I could still hear him via a twig cracking sharply and a slithering rumble of stones. That persuaded me take an even steeper ascent—although I did ask Benjamin first whether he thought he could manage it.

Sean had already raced ahead and was looking down at us in four-legged superiority and with a canine version of impatience. I saw Ben glance sharply at his beloved dog, about to shout to him to come to heel—then close his mouth as he thought better of it.

The boy was obviously out of breath. That didn't make me feel very good. As a matter of fact I was working up quite a brew of guilt over Benjamin, one way and another. His now-grass-stained pants were in front of me at this point. I recollect seeing his thin little legs stiffen as he climbed higher, and I also remember telling myself we must have a discreet chat before he unburdened every aspect of our expedition to his mother. I think it is because children are such *blabbermouths* I tend to treat them with prudence.

Then I fell. For a moment I relived the incident on the Cornish moors with the tip-truck and the quarry railway—I guess it was still fresh in memory. Blackness descended and I knew nothing more until I grew aware of fierce light, a mallet thudding pegs in my head; and my godson's anxious voice.

Sometimes—and that day was one of them—I feel my own mind is a stranger to the rest of me. For instance, persuaded that I'd suffered a nasty fall from the slippery terrain we were climbing, I managed to focus enough energy into the incredible labour of getting my hurting body out of the crevice into which I'd fallen.

Slowly, step after aching step, I climbed once more to the level reaches of the dark forest.

Not that I would've been capable of this if it hadn't been for the physical support as well as steady encouragement of that beloved little boy. His voice had taken on a gentleness as he'd put both hands to my elbow, allowing bushes and saplings to whip at him, as he pioneered a path through the thick brush at the base of giant Douglas firs.

"Come on, Uncle Davey. This way. No—over here. It isn't much further. Mind that root! See that stump? You'll be all right, Uncle Davey. I bet we both look a sight when we get home!" If he was scared by the sight of me he was doing a damn good job at covering up. Perhaps in the Murphy household it paid an only child to often look impassive.

A ten-year-old boy and his aging dog, helping a stricken man in his early forties through intractable woodland. It is easy to wince at the sentiment, but I'd be less than truthful if I didn't record the pride—no, *devotion* isn't too strong a word—his loving care sprang in me that spring day.

When, incredibly, he finally helped me into the auto and I drove us slowly to his home, the tears behind my eyes were as much for him as reaction to the razor pain in my chest and upper left leg.

I sank on to the sofa in the Murphys' living room. Jacqueline was all efficient concern as she listened to her son's account of the accident, eased off my shirt and undid my belt before starting on my mud-stained jeans. I saw Benjamin pause in his narrative to stare down at me. I knew self-consciousness, even then.

Jacqueline intercepted the exchange. "Go and give Sean a good towelling, darling, and see he has water. I'm sure he's terribly thirsty."

When he'd gone she felt my thigh and I winced. "You hurt there? In your leg?" I nodded wanly. "Let me have a look," she said evenly. "Just try and ease up a little bit." I wasn't quite sure what she intended but her firmness controlled my frailty. I curved my spine: gingerly raised my waist. Before I really comprehended her motives, with one deft movement she'd lowered my jeans and underpants, leaving my frontal intimacies flopped before her.

That was the best part of fifteen years ago—yet it is still a hard thing to describe. I was in pain, weak, indeed, worn out from the labours of trudging through the depths of that forest. Even so, my sense of outrage at a woman staring at my genitals outweighed everything—including all the little prudish proprieties I'd felt in Benjamin's presence. I thought suddenly of closety Gordon and of how many forms one's sexual vulnerability can take.

I think she sensed my self-consciousness because her eyes never focussed as they surveyed me. Nor did her voice reveal anything but objectivity. "I can't see any abrasions, Davey. There's no sign of swelling." I saw no humour then in *that* comment!

"Maybe lower down," I said thickly. "It hurts there, too. Maybe the leg's broken."

Very lightly, with her fingertips, she touched me in the fleshy part of my inner thigh. "Just there?" she asked. I could've screamed like an outraged virgin as her knuckles innocently brushed my scrotum. But I didn't. I simply shook my head instead. "Well, there's a bruise lower down, and another on your shin. But they don't seem enough. . . . "

She straightened suddenly. "I'm going to call the doctor. We won't play amateur guess games." With that she left for the kitchen and the telephone.

She'd scarcely turned behind my back before I'd grabbed my pants and underwear and restored them to their normal positions. I felt better immediately. At the prospect of the doctor's arrival I had less and less discomfort from either my rib cage or my leg. I tried to grin when Jacqueline returned to say the physician was on his way.

"It's like the toothache," I explained. "The tooth feels better and better all the way to the dentist."

"I don't think I'll ever make you out," she said slowly, as she sat down opposite.

"Why?"

"I can understand your shyness—being a little embarrassed, even. But with your best friend! And you obviously hurt! Does my being a woman bother you *that* much?"

I took a pusillanimous route. "Jacqueline, I really don't feel well. Can we leave the parlor psychiatry until later?"

She shrugged. "I'm sorry. It just popped out. Then it isn't every day a woman has a male flinch over his penis and balls when he's had a nasty accident. And I *am* French, remember!"

I closed my eyes and refused to open them until I heard her close the door quietly behind her. I thought I heard Benjamin's voice some time after that—and grimaced at the thought of her telling him why she'd told him to leave the room.

I think I must have dozed off for when I next opened my eyes and saw Jacqueline again she was in the company of Owen Hearst, a family friend of the Murphys as well as our shared doctor. When he had examined me and asked me lots of questions, he stood looking down, the arm of his spectacles in his mouth, and a frown contracting his eyebrows.

"I should forget all about falling down that crevice and collecting a few bruises. It looks to me like you've had a slight heart attack. Shan't know for certain until I get you down to St. Paul's, which is where I want to see you next. I'm going to call an ambulance."

His diagnosis proved correct. I had had a small cardiac arrest according to the ECG an hour or so later. After I'd been examined by a whole slew of white-coated strangers—none of whom sparked the self-consciousness Jacqueline had—I finally lay quiet in my hospital bed. In spite of corporate assurances that what had occurred had to be treated as a warning rather than as a significant threat, my thoughts were somber. I had seen Ken and swiftly noted the worry in his eyes as I lay there. For the first time I could remember, I mulled my mortality.

"Little man, you've had a busy day," I said aloud to the white wall beyond my iron bed. "You ain't kidding!" I replied to my own remark. I cracked a smile. I was enjoying talking to myself as I lay there in the silent room. "I'm glad, though, that Ben was with me when that stud cruised me. If I'd been all alone and we'd made it there in the bushes—who knows, it might not have been such a slight heart attack after all!"

I must've talked louder than I'd intended for suddenly a stiff white nurse was at my side. "Is there anything I can get you?" she asked firmly.

I pretended I'd been talking in my sleep and stared dreamily up at her. "Thank you, but there's nothing I need. This has been a day when *not* having things done to me has probably paid off."

She seemed relieved not to have to run some errand for me. "Then try and get some sleep, Mr.Bryant. Tomorrow will be a busy day for you. Lots of tests for one thing," she called over her shoulder.

SEVEN

≈

In conjunction with the news about my heart condition I had a weird kind of delayed reaction. By my third day in hospital I was convinced I'd almost died when in the forest with Benjamin. Those who visited me in hospital were all highly solicitous, even grave.

Ken told me one afternoon that over twenty people had called asking for my hospital room and whether I could be visited. I really marvelled at the benison of friends but it was also a time when I learned of the huge variations in fear over one of our century's most prominent sicknesses.

AIDS, of course, would eventually create a unity of attitudes involving both bafflement, anguish and personal dread—but that was a horror still buried in the unfathomable future.

It was an era exuding an uneasy amalgam of science and superstition—much talk of hypodermics and horoscopes. Visitor after visitor evoked signs of the Zodiac and I felt like telling the nurse to add the fact I was a Leo to my medical chart at the end of my bed.

With the advent of Jacqueline and Neil, who arrived, the former flower-laden, the latter ashen-faced, I was at least spared puerile chatter over horoscopes. They sparred instead over whether she'd bought the right kind of flowers! When Helen and Gordon arrived with Ken, followed by the Inces, Neil at once did an imitation of me in twenty years time. It turned out to be a cross between a village idiot and Monty Wooley's movie performance in *The Man Who Came to Dinner.* Jacqueline interrupted him to enquire whether my sex life would be subsequently affected by the heart attack. As I lay there grinning at the reassuring predictability of my friends, Helen and Freddy Ince announced they both thought I should write a cookbook for cardiac cases. Only Ken and Gordon Goddard were quiet.

I was fortunate. In a week I was out of the hospital, and even the domestic convalescence Owen Hearst assured me was much shorter than he suggested for most of his patients. However, I did give up smoking altogether then and began the brisk early morning walks which have since become staples of my life.

From the time I returned home and began to pick up the threads of normal existence I can't honestly say I felt particularly unwell—and I certainly didn't feel old. But I did have a sense of a landmark reached and passed. There was one other corollary to that heart attack. It seemed to be a *contagious* malady! Within a fortnight of my leaving St. Paul's, Helen entered Vancouver General for an hysterectomy, and Jacqueline had her gall bladder removed the following month.

The third inheritor of my misfortune was the most worrisome. Gordon started to behave in a bizarre way. I was first aware of something amiss when Helen phoned me from a public call box. She suggested a late evening visit to the Sandbox, her favourite gay bar at the time. But the prospect of the musical din, the elbow-to-elbow crowding and the resultant heat was somewhat daunting. Instead, I suggested an inexpensive Italian restaurant by the beach.

I was being cunning. Helen, by this time, was a devotee of gay bars in Vancouver. But if she loved the steady thump of a musical beat, the fractured light of mirrored globes turning and the frenzied dancing on the apron-size dance floor, she adored being taken out to dinner even more.

I sensed immediately she didn't have a foursome in mind. Otherwise she wouldn't have mentioned a gay bar. Gordon still refused to be seen in one with her and when I informed her Ken was marking term papers she didn't demur.

She was heaping spaghetti and meatballs onto the plate of a ravenous young Derek when I collected her. Beneath her apron I noted she'd already changed for the evening. She patted her hair as she addressed me.

"If I'd known where we were going earlier you could've eaten here with us. We'll probably be having the same thing at Mario's, anyway."

I knew that was simply talk. There was no comparison for her between dining *à deux* in candlelight with a man—a waiter in attendance—and fretting over her unmistakably bland English cooking in her own kitchen.

"There's more in the saucepan," she told her son. "Only leave a bit for your Dad—if he should decide to come home at a reasonable hour.

Then to your homework, my lad. Davey and I won't be late so you can wait up, all right?"

Derek nodded, his mouth full of pasta. She bent over and kissed his ketchupy mouth. He half-turned in avoidance and took the opportunity to wave goodbye to me. For a brief moment I thought his raised hand flickered and dipped downwards—but I banished the image as the fruit of a corrupt imagination.

When we were out of earshot, at the elevator entrance, Helen turned to me. "I bet the little devil has that TV set on before we've reached your car! There's some campy British comedian on who Derek loves to imitate. He's shy with you but when we're alone he has me in stitches."

I made no reply—too full of thoughts about that limp-wristed adieu. Instead I smiled and nodded encouragingly, before changing the subject. "Gordon working late these days, then?" I knew he'd recently been given a promotion and now held a fairly senior position in the PR department.

"God knows what he's doing! That's the reason you're here. Has he been over to see you and Ken?"

I told her we hadn't seen her husband for a couple of weeks. Actually, Ken had seen Gordon with a rather rough looking type in the Castle. But as neither of us had spoken with him I felt the suppression justified.

We were driving along Marine Drive when Helen said something which startled me. "I know all about his visits to the steambaths, you know."

"No, I didn't know. That's to say—does he?"

"You don't have to play dumb. I couldn't care less—as long as he doesn't bring his tricks back home or embarrass his son. I'd kill him if did that!"

"I'm sure he's more worried than you are. He told me as much in California. Does he know *you* know, by the way?"

"He must. He can't come to bed at five a.m. smelling of chlorine or whatever, without realizing I know where he's been."

"Is that what's bothering you?"

"Davey! You're not listening! I've already said I don't care what he does at the tubs—provided it stays there. We haven't had sex for ages—you must realize that."

I hadn't. But I declined to admit it. "It seems you're managing a lot better than some couples. These mixed marriages aren't easy."

"*I* am managing," she interjected. "I don't think Gordon is." Her tone of voice gave me pause. She was alluding to something more disturbing than her husband's sex life.

"He's been promoted again, you know. His income's nearly doubled. We could now afford a really nice place to live and move out of that crummy apartment. Derek could easily go to UBC after high school and I could quit my part-time job at the bank."

"So things are on the up and up. Congratulations!"

"Are you kidding? Gordon wants to quit the phone company! He wants to go to UBC and do a BA, then an MA, and then a PHD, for Chrissakes! He wants to start his whole fucking life all over again! At the tender age of thirty-seven. And to hell with Derek and me!"

We were almost at the restaurant. I glanced at her. She wasn't far from tears.

"Let Ken talk to him," I said quickly. "He knows more about these university things than I do. Besides, he's a better listener."

I told Ken the minute I got home from a dismal meal at which Helen refused to talk any more of Gordon—though he patently remained the genesis of our glum thoughts and weighted mood.

The result was Ken called Gordon at work the next day. The first intimation that there was something seriously wrong with him was apparent within minutes of his arrival that same evening.

We were both working in the yard. I had embarked on the removal of two bamboo clumps—a task which quickly proved excessive and had me sweaty, headachy, and half-expecting another heart attack before I slumped into a chair. My lover had mown two lawns and retied roses on their respective trellises before joining me, when a car drew up and our dogs barked. We called for Gordon to join us under the wisteria.

It was a June evening and the sun was still strong. Ken asked him whether he preferred a chair in the shade by ours but our guest ignored the question. He just stood there, slim-figured and waistcoated in his dark city suit, staring down at us but somehow not seeing us.

He never once made eye contact. Nor did we verbally communicate much either.

"Congratulations on the promotion," I said.

"I know why Becky Sharp hates Amelia Sedley," he replied. "It's why I hate Helen. With too much goodness you suffocate."

I looked fondly at Ken. "Then I must suffocate, too," I said brightly.

"My God! Look at the time!" Ken said. "The yard arm and all that. How about joining us for a drink, Gordon? It's been thirsty work out here in the yard."

"Gordon likes a gin and tonic," I said.

"I know all about good and evil," Gordon announced. "And I know more about the nineteenth century novel than either of you."

Ken looked uncomfortable. "You do indeed," he muttered.

"And I know more about getting drinks," I supplied, standing up to do just that.

"I should be a full professor. I shall start giving lectures." Gordon laughed loudly, excessively. "What I need is a banyan tree. I've not only gotten rusty working downtown but morally filthy. I need to be cleansed by the clear waters of intellect. That's why I'm so glad I did all that grad research before I emigrated. I'm finally going to put my doctorate to use. I start on Monday, you know. *The Nature of Evil in the 19th-Century Novel.* How's that, eh?"

I sat down again.

"That's a marvelous idea, Gordon," Ken told him. "You might offer a series for the Extension Department next fall. I'm sure I could help. Okay?"

Gordon didn't look at all happy. Instead he scowled and kept clenching his hands. If his academic fabrications were strange they were nothing compared to what followed.

"I'm going to dig a pit," he said. He crossed to the spade I'd dropped against the trellis after removing the bamboo clumps. "A grave for sinners. It will be all dark down there. The colour of our sins. We're all damned, we queers. You know that, of course?"

"Then now's the time to eat, drink and be merry. You'll stay for supper?" I asked.

But Gordon was beyond such diversion. He began to sob. If you listened hard you could make out words as he scooped his hole. "All flesh must rot. . . . Only the next generation . . . Derek can find purity. We're spoiled . . . bodies defiled. My flesh must turn to soil and start all over again."

"I think he might hurt himself," I suggested quietly. But Ken had anticipated me. He was already halfway across the lawn. I crossed over to Gordon, put my arm about him. Just as in Monterey, he cradled his weeping head against my shoulder and shook in his grief. I was so pathetically ignorant of mental distress. So *helpless.* It was like looking at death. A baffled sense of bereavement.

How long we sat there in the quiet of the garden amid lengthening shadows, I've no idea. We didn't move until Owen Hearst arrived in response to Ken's summons and giving our friend a pill, drove a pliant Gordon off in his car.

EIGHT

≈

According to Owen Hearst, Gordon might not have stayed more than two or three days in the psychiatric unit of St. Vincent's but on his second night he attempted to hang himself in the bathroom. He was transferred to Riverview where he spent the following two months.

Neither Ken nor I visited him there—Helen asked us not to—and I never did get to learn the precise nature of the treatment he underwent. But when he was home once more and back at work, although now more content with his job (never again referring to a change to an academic career) he seemed a more resigned person. He lived far more in Helen's vortex and when we took up regular weekly visits again with the Goddards, Gordon would be smilingly present—but only just. . . .

According to his wife he now attended the steambaths more frequently than ever before. He was equally diligent in going on North Shore mountain hikes, fishing trips up the Squamish Valley, and even attending hockey games, with his sixteen-year-old son. That was the time, too, when he both stopped smoking and became a teetotaller. When the four of us were making summer vacation plans that Christmas and I suggested we all five go to Europe, Gordon surprised us by quietly but firmly declining. He thought the idea a perfect one for Helen and Derek as Ken and I could show them a France they'd never seen. With the language at our disposal, he argued, it would make an altogether different kind of holiday than they could have on their own. It was finally agreed that, after visiting relatives in England, mother and son would meet up with us in Paris.

Something else was to happen that spring, though, which would have considerable impact upon those vacation plans. Neil Murphy, whose conduct on campus, Ken grumbled, was progressively outrageous, became involved in a nasty scandal.

I had driven out to UBC one blustery day. It was a Friday when I usually collected Ken after his final class. Heading west, I took the route skirting empty beaches rather than the speedier highway. It is easy to be retrospectively prescient but the fact is I nursed some vague tension that day and hankered for the sight of uninterrupted sand and sea across to the snow-capped peaks of the North Shore.

I could see no ships at anchor, no persons trudging the smooth tracts of sand. The absence of life was a balm. We were coming to an end of that introspective time of year when the Rockies acted as a barrier, the rains enveloped us, and we enjoyed our seclusion without the scrutiny of tourists.

The bay, in its gray and glassy calm, was more evocative of a lake than the open sea. As I drove close to its mildly frothing edge I was quite captivated by its melancholy.

The mood was shattered as I opened a seventh-floor door to greet an agitated roommate who informed me he'd just been visited by a distraught Neil. He'd been caught an hour earlier by the campus police, *flagrante delicto*, in a toilet—in the company of a half-naked student who'd been allowed to go after providing his name and address.

Neil had been detained considerably longer—while some uniformed oaf had laboriously taken down a highly fictitious account of professorial bowel problems and the kindness of a young man coming to his cubicle when he had groaned for aid.

The trouble was—as he had disconsolately informed Ken—there'd been no time to collaborate with the youngster over an agreed story, so the kid would thus be entirely unaware of any purported stomach ailment or request by Neil to examine his hind parts owing to pains in the area of his kidneys.

The cold facts were, Neil explained, any possible impression of a young Good Samaritan conducting a medical survey, was wholly vitiated by the highly visible display of two emphatic erections as the cops had burst in.

That tell-tale piece of evidence of sexual hanky-panky (in a notorious campus location) had been further compounded by the positioning of the engineering student's member at the portal of Neil's buttocks as if *it* were striving for a measure of interior investigation.

The faces of both cops had remained impassive during Neil's elaborate explanation but he was left, nevertheless, with the sinking feeling they didn't believe a word of it. Worse, he confessed to Ken, were the remarks of the older of the two officers that there was ample evidence for a charge of seducing a minor as well as the committing of an obscene act in a public place.

Only his academic standing, they informed him, delayed his arrest and their taking him away. They would be notifying the Dean of Arts and the head of his department of what had taken place and he would be hearing from the RCMP as to what proceedings would be taken. He had fled straight to Ken's office after the burly pair had driven off, and completely broken down after jerkily relating his reconstruction of the embarrassing events.

For my part, I was quite distressed over Ken. I had rarely seen him so agitated for any reason. That stirred the most hostile thoughts about the unfortunate Neil, even while I guiltily identified with his current plight.

"Where the hell is he now?" I asked, not bothering to conceal the irritation. Ken didn't seem aware of it.

"Back in his office with the door shut. He says he can't bear to see anyone. He wants me to drive him home as he's afraid of being alone in the car. I'm supposed to call Jacqueline and give her a laundered version of what happened. He doesn't feel up to dropping a bombshell the minute he arrives home. I can't blame him for that."

"In fact the only thing Neil seems up to is cruising a notorious john in his backyard and then fooling around with jail bait! I ask you!"

I wasn't asking Ken anything. I was covertly addressing myself. I had surveyed those same toilets where Neil had been caught—and only a few weeks earlier. So perhaps I would have been a little more cautious but could I honestly say I would have done much about ascertaining a precise age?

As I watched Ken arrange and rearrange the already neat pile of papers upon his desk, my self-questioning went further. Why the hell did the likes of Neil and Davey risk so much for casual sex in public places? What was it that drove us to go against all prudence or plain common sense? Why risk all the things we cherished most—our families and partners, and their trust and loyalty? Was it some peculiar gay flirtation with disaster: a deep-rooted masochism or need to embrace doom? I had no answers and that only increased my irrational annoyance with Neil for letting us all down and providing cant-ridden Fundamentalists with spurious ammunition.

I tried to conceal such feelings from Ken—which was a waste of time. "I can't think what he thought he was doing. I can imagine Benjamin's face on learning his Dad was caught being buggered by someone hardly older than himself."

"Come off it, Davey! Since when has that influenced anyone doing anything? I think Neil needs your help—not your moralizing." My lover actually glowered at me. "Jesus! You can be irritating at times! Can't you see I'm up to my neck in this?"

"What I can see is Ken Bradley playing super-queen again. I guess I'm just an unfortunate interruption of your lady-bountiful act with that irresponsible faggot!"

"Please quit the name-calling. It doesn't help anyone and it leaves you in a somewhat vulnerable, not to say hypocritical, position. Are you saying you've *never* cruised a public can? Or picked up an under-aged kid?"

That was dirty pool. Ken knew just how hard I had struggled over the years to put those impulses behind me. "Just like you to bring things back to me when it's Neil we're supposed to be talking about. I'm not stupid. Nor are our friends. We've all noticed how you jump to Neil's defense if he's criticized. Half of UBC believes you two are lovers because you spend so much time together out here."

He suddenly looked haggard. "Don't be ridiculous! Forget yourself for a few seconds. One of our closest friends is in a terrible jam. *Neil could end up in jail.* Doesn't that mean anything to you? If not, then think of Jacqueline and Benjamin and the pain and shame facing them."

"That's precisely who I was thinking of while you were preaching at me! If you'd come down sometime from your perch you'd discover that lots of us are capable of thinking things through for ourselves."

Ken got up from behind his desk. "This isn't getting us anywhere. Why don't you go to Neil's office and comfort him a bit. But no bitching, mind, or telling him how stupid he's been."

"I've no intention of taking over your role," I said.

He shrugged, resolute as ever in his refusal to spar. "While you're with him I'll call Leon Eichelbaum in the law faculty. He isn't gay but he's very *sympathique.* I'll also talk to Owen Hearst—it might be as well to have a doctor in on things to say Neil's been under strain or something."

I wasn't in the mood to listen to my lover masterfully pulling strings on behalf of anyone—let alone Neil whom I was now prepared to blame for causing one of the few intense flare-ups between Ken and me.

I left his office without saying another word. When I opened the door to Neil's and saw him hunched behind his desk, my irritation vanished at once. His phone lay on his desk, the receiver some way from its cradle. I could hear metallic sounds coming from it. In spite of the distortion and the faintness I knew it was Jacqueline's voice. He looked up at me, his eyes red from crying. His usually neat hair was in disarray. He shook his head at the phone and buried his face in his hands.

I understood. Crossing to the desk I picked up the receiver and softly said my name. Before she could reply I went on. "I've just got here, sweetheart. I've been with Ken and everything's in hand. I'll get back to you, okay? Now I'd better talk to Neil. We'll get him home soon—not to worry."

I let the receiver fall loudly back into place and crossed round the desk. I half crouched over him. He suddenly lifted his head and placed it against the hardness of my ribs. I was fleetingly reminded of Gordon and his recent distress.

For a very long time there was nothing but the rhythmic sound of his breathing. I stroked his curly hair back into place and felt the wetness of his cheek against my fingers. When he spoke his voice was so muffled I had to bend awkwardly down to hear.

"I was on my way home. On the way to the car park when I suddenly thought . . . I didn't really expect anyone to be there . . . late on a Friday afternoon . . . at this time of year. . . . Oh, Christ, Davey, what could I have been thinking about!"

I held his head even tighter. "I promised Ben I'd take him to the theater tonight to see *The Cherry Orchard.* She didn't want to go so there'd be just the two of us. I told him it was my favourite play—that's why he wanted to see it with me."

He started to cry again.

"Don't, Neil," I murmured.

"He won't want to see me, now—let alone go with me to a fucking play!"

"You've got to trust him. Trust both of them. He's the son of a Dubliner and a Lyonnaise isn't he? So he knows what loyalty is!"

I sensed he was trying hard to control himself while his face remained hidden under my arm. "He's still only a child. Christ, I should've never laid a trip like that on him! I truly deserve to go to jail, Davey!"

"Which would make things better? For Benjamin and Jacqueline?"

Neil finally stared up at me. "What am I to do, then? You've got to help me."

"We'll think of something," I said, happy in the confidence that with Ken's persistent practicality and one of my bright ideas we would do just that. In the meantime, Ken would call the lawyer and I would hold his hand. . . .

On the way to his home—after I had bolstered his courage over meeting Jacqueline and Benjamin—I sat in back with him while Ken drove and told us how supportive both Leon Eichelbaum and Owen Hearst had proved to be. He said that Leon felt that it would be unlikely the matter would get beyond the university. I gave Neil a squeeze as I felt him sag with relief at those words.

It wasn't all plain-sailing though. When we got to the Murphys' home, Benjamin was out there in the front yard awaiting us, his old setter, Sean (sharing the boy's seventeenth year), standing at his side. My godson had developed an expression which was wholly alien to both his parents. He could look quite impassive and join this inscrutability with an inert physical stance that sat oddly on a teenager.

Ken and I felt sure this demeanour had been carefully choreographed over the years as a means to escape siding with either parent in one of their numerous conflicts. He went into one of these almost catatonic fits until the parental storm blew over. He thus confronted us now.

Neil was between us as we walked up the path towards the front door. "Hi, Benjie," he called, forcing a smile. His son didn't budge, even though we passed no more than four feet from him. Nor did words escape him. Sean slowly wagged his tail, but squatted stiffly on his haunches when it was obvious we were not going to approach and pat him.

I took up the rear as we entered. I glanced back. Benjamin took one look in our direction before making for the street, shoulders slumped dejectedly, his grizzled setter trailing behind him. I wanted to pursue and explain the inexplicable.

From the interior came Jacqueline's voice, a rasp of hysteria to it. There was no doubt where the priority lay. I was keenly aware of how depleted Neil was—a fresh savaging from her would be disastrous.

I attempted to warn her. "It's been quite an afternoon for old Neil, here. I gather from Ken that Owen Hearst is on his way with some kind of sedative."

She watched us, arms akimbo, as we walked across the living room and sat down on each side of him on the sofa.

"You don't mean to tell me he's been in an *accident* as well as an *incident*?"

"Just what he told you on the phone, Jackie," Ken said quietly. "No more and no less."

"Then perhaps it is me who needs Owen?" she retorted. "I'd include Benjamin—but after what he's going through I think he's more in need of a psychiatrist."

"Poor little bastard," Neil said. "He must be going through hell."

"Pity you didn't think of that before you went child-molesting," his wife said roughly.

I stiffened. "Let's not over-react. You know bloody well Neil's no chicken queen. You're both going to have to be pretty cool over this business—for Benjamin's sake as well as your own."

Ken had already gotten to his feet. "If this is mutual recrimination time then we are best away. But I'll tell you Jackie what I've already told Neil. We're your friends. We are here to help. For goodness' sake, give us a call. We'll be right over. If you'd like Ben to come with us while you discuss things with Owen and Leon we'd be only too happy to have him."

Jacqueline looked sullen—although I had a suspicion tears weren't far away. After all, I knew her very well. Better, perhaps, than I knew Neil.

"You don't understand at all. Then why should you? You aren't a mother. Not even a proper spouse. When I've lost my husband I don't want my child out of my sight. He's all I've got. He's the only thing meaningful I've got left."

"God! I've hurt you, haven't I?" whispered Neil.

"I understand," I said, as we made to go. "You're over-simplifying as always, but I understand."

Ken slowed down as he passed her, stopped in fact. If he had looked unhappy and drawn on campus, he now looked tortured. "You haven't really *got* him, have you? He's no one's possession."

With that faintly prophetic remark we left the Murphys to await events.

NINE

≈

I wasn't privy, of course, to the daily exchanges between Neil and Jacqueline after his apprehension by the campus police. Nor were either of us given opportunity to learn the particulars of whatever hell young Benjamin had to undergo. That was as well. Families can benefit from suffering their wounds in private—without recourse to all the remorseless goodwill which both friends and society are so eager to unleash.

I know that's an unfashionable thing to say. Then modishness has never been my strong suit. And as I am of those who prefer to retreat to the dark of a lair to lick my wounds it would ill behove me to counsel others differently.

I stayed clear of the Murphys from respect, not pusillanimity. I wasn't surprised to hear—on learning that no charges were to be preferred and that a severe reprimand by the Campus RCMP sergeant and the Faculty Administration were to be the official price-tags for Neil's erotic antics—that Jacqueline decided to take Benjamin to visit his grandparents in Lyons early that summer. It was left open whether they would eventually return to the Murphy home.

When Ken told me of the French plans for Jacqueline and my godson I telephoned to ask whether they'd be interested in joining us with Helen and Derek. Jacqueline proved amiability itself. There was no hint of the friction between her and Neil which flared as mutual recrimination (Ken still being my informant from his talks with Neil) on virtually a daily basis. She and Ben would be delighted to meet with us all in Lyons and why didn't we plan to spend some time in the region where she would be only too happy to act as our guide?

Ken and I went one further and successfully sounded out Neil and Gordon about sharing Neil's house while their wives and sons were away. Helen thought that a splendid notion as Gordon could repaint the apartment and not have to spend his nights amid the debris of cans and brushes. I'm sure she was also thinking it would be a welcome alternative to his being left on his own—with the less certain corollary that Neil's presence might save her husband from the temptations of steambaths or late night cruising of the city's parks. . . .

By the time Ken and I arrived in Paris the two Goddards had already been visiting Helen's parents in Somerset for three weeks. From a brief note awaiting us at our friend's apartment, both the small market town of Frome, and the cranky couple (who had taken an immediate dislike to their grandson) had already exhausted their charm for the Canadian visitors.

Helen followed a detailed description of a flaming row with her emphysemic father over her indulgence of Derek by concluding her sprawled letter with the sentiment that her son might be guilty of geriatricide if he had to spend more time with his grandparents.

They were heading for London where Helen had a cousin, and would it be possible for them to join us in Paris a littler earlier than we had initially arranged? She had carefully added her cousin's phone number.

After emptying our bags and inspecting the spacious apartment on the rue Berlioz—which Ken's old friend, Yves, had kindly left us while away on television business in Mauritius—we sortied out onto the Avenue Victor Hugo and made in the direction of the Etoile.

We were only a block or so from the house in which we had first met, and we were both quiet as memories jostled for space over long-gone youth, student enthusiasms, and the engulfing bliss of falling in love during those sun-shot September days.

At the top of the Avenue d'Iéna we found a bench and sat watching the traffic swirl about the Arc de Triomphe. "There's much more now than in 1951," I remarked to my lover. "And isn't everything louder than it was?"

"Memory softens," Ken said. "It also distorts. I can only think of you wearing a beret, smoking blue gauloises, and our listening to endless 78s by Jean Sablon and Tino Rossi. We *must* have done more than that, and you didn't spend the *whole* time trying to look more French than the French in those laced pigskin gloves!"

I changed the subject. "This isn't the Paris we met in, you realize?"

Ken shrugged. "Nowhere's ever the same years later. If *we've* altered, why shouldn't Paris have changed, too?"

A myriad irritations surged in me—charged largely, I recognized, by Helen's cryptic note. "That's silly! Of course I'm talking about degree. Some cities alter more than others. Just like people." I adopted my measured tones designed for the slow-witted. "Fifth Avenue hasn't changed as much as the *Champs Elysées.* Just look at this traffic swirling round the *Etoile.* It was just an empty space for so much of the time in 1951. Frankly, I don't like Paris nowadays. I'll be glad when we're out of it. I suppose we'll be bogged down for days, sight-seeing with Derek and his mother."

"Who says so? That was never part of the plan." Ken sounded surprised. "We head south as soon as they arrive."

"That's not what I read from her letter. They want to come early and we'll have to entertain them here for a while. We can't upset the arrangements with Jacqueline down in Lyons. Personally, I can't wait to get there."

I suspect Ken thought a change of prospect might bring a change of mind for me. "Let's stroll down the *Avenue du Bois,*" he suggested, using the old name for the Avenue Foch. I rose from the bench as he did. The din of traffic and stench of gasoline made anywhere else preferable.

We hadn't gone very far before we passed a resplendent English pram—replete with silvery tassels hanging from its sun canopy and containing a cooing infant sprawled on soft white pillows. My vexatious mood evaporated. It wasn't that I felt particularly drawn to babies (indeed, a particular affectation of mine was to dismiss them as too prone to diaper reek) but the sight of that expensive vehicle of infancy propelled properly by, I assumed by the starched uniform and red cheeks, a bona fide English nanny, stirred a calming nostalgia in me.

The young woman with stiff white cuffs and matching headdress, the baby clutching a rattle, were welcome insignia of past journeying down that thoroughfare; when Ken and I had sighed in the pale green light from street lamps filtering through fanned chestnut leaves.

Back then, with fall leaves changing colour, the nannies had been vigorously pushing their charges home—presumably to opulent nurseries and that ambience of riches, which, in our radical youth, we had opted to condemn.

Not so now. It was a reassurance that spring afternoon, with the virginally fresh chestnuts scarcely screening the mansions that lay far behind them, that the rich still held sway on that sumptuous *allée*. Pressed, I guess I would've argued that their wealthy presence was equally balanced by the poor of other *arrondissements* than the posh Sixteenth—and that if the two ever met head on, we'd be back to 1789 and thus recycling history.

Further down the gentle slope towards the *Bois de Boulogne* we chanced upon a sight which again struck nostalgia in me. Only this time for quite different reasons and from quite another venue.

Sauntering slowly towards us was a group of four: a middle-aged couple with, apparently, their two teenaged children. There was nothing vaguely familiar about either the man and woman or the pony-tailed girl. But Ken and I exchanged glances when the youth passed us. He not only physically resembled young Ned Ince, the son of Freddy and Joan, but also struck our practised eyes as being potentially gay.

There was that giveaway glance towards us which resulted immediately in a lowering of eyes and a self-conscious blush. His walk was more springy than most, and his slim wrist bore an elegant band. Two fingers supported rings of extravagant size. Beyond all that was the voice we heard as he passed. The French pitch is higher than those of the English-speaking worlds. But those flutey tones owed nothing to the French tongue. As we discussed the similarity of his features to those of young Ned—we also concluded that although perhaps he was not yet aware of it, there was little doubt of the route he was travelling.

We then talked, as we had hundreds of times before, of the mystery in the instant recognition gays experienced between each other.

The faint reminder of Ned evoked Derek and his mother. Now in a more amenable frame of mind, I agreed with Ken that we should call them that evening and invite them to stay in Yves' large apartment as soon as they wanted.

'Soon' proved to be right away. Only twenty-four hours elapsed before we found ourselves waiting for the London flight at the *Aérogare des Invalides* for mother and son. Derek was the first to alight from the blue airport bus. I immediately registered the jeans and short-sleeved cotton shirt. Perhaps it was the cut of them but in conjunction with his shaped haircut, he stood out prominently as a North American. As I subsequently told one of Ken's ex-students—if you think because they all wear jeans, yours are some kind of camouflage—forget it!

For the first time I was made distinctly aware of how tall he was. Even as an eighteen-year-old he now dwarfed both parents. He stood at the bottom step politely awaiting the descent of his mother. She appeared bedecked in summery white garments I'd never seen her wear in Vancouver. I decided they'd all been bought for the trip and wondered fleetingly which stores she'd patronized for both of them as her strapping son was also obviously in new clothes.

Smugly, I reflected that neither Ken nor I had purchased a single shirt for our vacation but I grudgingly conceded she was always a careful shopper and that her equally frugal husband was currently repainting their apartment—at a saving of several hundred dollars.

I had rarely seen Helen looking more happy and relaxed than when we embraced, screamed mutual greetings, and bundled into the cab Ken commandeered. To our questions over Gordon she informed us she'd spoken with him the previous evening and that he had been calling the two of them at her parents' place in Somerset quite regularly since their departure.

He was feeling very well, she said, and even enjoying the painting project while he was *fellow-bacheloring* with Neil. There was no mention of his mental health and, certainly, neither Ken nor I were about to bring it up.

After dinner that evening at a small restaurant near the hotel we four sat at a *brasserie* just off the Etoile and watched the crowds saunter by. I distinctly remember the scent of lindens on the warm night air and ponderously explaining to Derek that linden trees were Britishly known as limetrees and had no connection whatever with the citrus fruit.

I became so involved in my botany lesson that it was too late before I eventually noticed the boy's features grow wooden in boredom and I finally ground to a halt.

In contrast, Helen and Ken chatted away with great animation as she fervently expressed her enthusiasm for the warm May Paris evening—with my roommate concurring and throwing in references to our youthfully shared days in the French capital.

Derek remained silent after my protracted lime spiel—his immature features still stony, I thought, as he stared out at what for him must've been a wholly alien scene. I wondered if he was actively disliking what he was observing and wishing he were back with his coevals in Vancouver.

The notion grated. "Has Ken told you we've heard from Jacqueline?" I asked Helen, breaking in on their conversation. "Her situation's a bit like yours was. She's dying to see us as she's getting more than a little bored with her parents in *Maison Blanche.* That's just a dreary suburb, you know."

"At least she's got Ben. I know from Old Moody there just what a *lifeline* a son can be!"

I thought fondly of the boy I was convinced had saved my life the year before. "How right you are—he's just the person to fend off the blues and to make her laugh if her parents get her down. Mind you, it's a marvelous opportunity for Benjamin, too. I mean for her to introduce her only son to her native land. He'll understand her all the more for that."

"Don't be naïve," Helen said comfortably. "Children by definition *never* understand their parents. In any case, she's brought Ben to France several times since he was a baby."

"Four," said Ken. "Three times with Neil, too."

I compressed lips and joined Derek in counting the cars—if that's what he was doing. Why did it irk me so when corrected by Ken? I mean so much *more* than when she did it—and that was aggravating enough. Something to do with our love and my sense he should be more loyal to me when she was around, I told myself.

I switched my attention back to Derek again. "It will be nice for you when we meet up with the Murphys. At least you'll have Benjamin and won't be stuck with us old fogeys."

The boy nodded vacantly—still staring at the unceasing flow of traffic.

"They won't exactly be boon companions," his mother contributed.

"After all, there is quite a gap in their ages. That means a lot when you're eighteen and he's younger, doesn't it, old lad?"

Her son seemed no more inclined to make common cause with her than the rest of us. " I like Ben all right," he said gruffly. "I prefer him to Ned Ince who's just a year *older*, not younger, than me by all but three months."

Ken looked quizzically at the teenager. " I would have thought he was older than you than that. In any case, I don't think we need to worry too much about bumping into the Inces here in France. Though Davey and I did think we saw Ned's double yesterday. He's with his parents. They've rented a trailer and are driving down to California for their vacation."

For the first time since he'd arrived in Paris, it seemed to me, a note of enthusiasm crept into the boy's response. "That'd be neat! They going right down to Big Sur like we did?"

"As I recall your chief interest being the purchase and consumption of ice cream," I said, "I'm surprised you even *remember* south of Carmel—'cause that's where the ice cream cones gave out. God! That was centuries ago!"

"Which means Derek is centuries older," his mother said quickly. "His interests have grown as much as his height."

"I steer clear of ice cream at the moment, Davey. It isn't good for my complexion. The same with candy."

Smugness sat ill on the young, I decided. I waved at the white-coated waiter. "I'd like a calvados as a night-cap," I informed the company. "Anyone for a postprandial liqueur?" But I had to drink alone.

I only had time to gulp the remains of the fiery drink before we embarked on a final stroll down the *Champs Elysées* and returned to the apartment for the night.

On the road next morning (Ken driving with Derek alongside, Helen in back with me) I questioned her about the time spent with her parents. I say *question*, but interrogation was hardly necessary. I had only to mention Somerset and she was off.

"You've no idea what perfectly dreadful people they've become."

"Dreadful?" I was out of practice with her absolutes—besides, a minuscule hangover provided a continuing vein of tension. "As bad as that?"

"Smug," she said heavily. "Beyond which nothing's worse! The whole bloody country is complacent—always was I suppose. But there's a peculiar Baptist attitude that my Dad has acquired *in toto.* He won't argue, won't even disagree, with a thing I say. Partly because I'm a bloody woman—and he's worse than blasted St. Paul over that—even if wild horses wouldn't drag it from him. I could put up with his patronizing of Mum and myself if it stopped there. It's the whole goddamn world beyond his stupid island."

Even Ken, apparently, felt called to remonstrate. "I think you'll find that's universal, my dear. No one thinks much beyond their own bailiwick. I mean, is there anyone worse than your typical Vancouver patriot?"

"At least there I don't have to be under the same roof with it," Helen countered. "And it's my *father* sitting there with his wet walrus moustache pretending he doesn't understand me if I use a North American term like *gas* or *truck.* Jesus! Davey, there were times I could've screamed at him for treating me like a retarded child who'd chosen to live with a bunch of savages who hadn't had the advantages of living in fucking Frome!"

"What about your mother? I thought she bugged you, too."

"You bet your life she did! Only with her it was through Derek. She never let the poor kid alone. When it wasn't 'Derek, please don't scuff the carpet,' or 'Derek, that chair wasn't made for rocking,' it was talking at me through him . . . 'How strange that your mother never feeds you apple dumplings and custard,' or, 'I suppose we shouldn't expect you to talk civilly to your grandparents if you speak the way you do to your mother.'

"It was endless. Not a day went by when she wasn't digging at him or playing that irritating false poverty game she so adores. 'Well, we can't afford fresh pineapple here, my boy.' Or 'I suppose you're used to those big flashy cars out there but here you'll have to get used to our little ones like every one else.' *Out there*, for Chrissakes! You'd think we lived in outer space the way she went on! I made a point of referring to 'out *here*' whenever I mentioned England."

"I don't mind if I never see Frome again," Derek suddenly volunteered.

"Come to that, I hope I've seen the last of Gran and Gramps as well. They're the pits."

"We're coming to Beaune next," our driver announced. "It'll be a good place for lunch—especially if we can find that super restaurant. Remember, Davey? The one the ananas came in a whole bucket of kirsch?"

I did but I wasn't minded to expatiate on the fact. I was feeling as sick and tired of all these carefully couched memories that Ken was stirring over our previous French visitations as I was of his ploys to avoid disagreement in the car. I launched into a spirited defense of Derek's detraction of Frome and his grandparents, taking his adolescent sulks one step further and seeking intellectual substance for them.

"I must say I loathed Frome when I lived near there as an evacuee during the war. I found the town insufferably provincial."

"You sound like a Viennese refugee from Hitler landing up in Prince George, B.C. with only a high school pipe band for musical sustenance. I guess even bagpipes are better than concentration camps." Ken's mouth was tight as he moved us into the slow lane prior to quitting the auto-route.

I wasn't surrendering that quickly. "Ken, it's not like you to make such ludicrous comparisons. I'm not complaining about Frome's brass band during World War II—I'm talking about a bully named Leslie Ralston who made me masturbate him in public on our way home from choir practice at Christ Church."

"I think I'd rather hear about that super restaurant," Helen said. "Schoolboy sex always sounds so *grotty*, doesn't it? At least for those of us who were never schoolboys."

"No worse than a bunch of girls talking about their periods," I snapped.

"Well, schoolgirl menstruation's hardly become a literary industry, has it, darling?"

"I suppose not," I retorted. "I imagine it's been superseded by *Sex With Daddy* which seems all the feminist rage nowadays."

"Let's save our women's lib battles until we meet up with Jacqueline," Ken suggested. "Then we'll be even in numbers."

"I'm starving," Derek contributed—either peevishly or diplomatically—I wasn't sure which. "What's the name of this super restaurant, Ken, that you and Davey enjoyed when you were young?"

"Le Coq d'Or," my lover supplied. "And we weren't exactly children when we were last there. It can be just as happy an experience for us now as it was then—provided we all make a bit of an effort."

Contrition stirred in me. "I had the best *rognons* I've ever tasted," I said. "And you, young man, are going to have the finest meal in your life, even without ice cream."

But in the event, although Derek ordered kidneys along with me, he left his virtually untouched. From Beaune on to Lyons he and his mother dozed and with my taking over from Ken as driver, as usual I spoke little. I think we were all rather relieved at the approaching prospect of joining up with the volatile Jacqueline and my beloved if somewhat unpredictable godson.

TEN

≈

As we entered the venerable ecclesiastical capital of France and I looked down on the confluent surges of the swirling Saône and eddying Rhône, my pulse quickened. I couldn't help it. It needed no Ken to remind me of the bittersweet past for this was a territory I'd entered even before my partner had pierced my life and rerouted my existence.

I'd first known the twin-river city when I was only a year or so older than our callow young passenger in the car—when, God knows, I'd been vastly different from this soft and suspicious product of western Canada's land of milk and honey.

Such somber brooding, as we sped past elegant bridges which, along with feathery acacia trees as boulevard fringes, helped to soften the massed stone of the sprawling city, did peculiar things to me.

Most of all it sparked a hunger for solitude. It wasn't very long after we'd duly met up with Jacqueline and my godson, that I managed to make an extended and lone excursion to half-forgotten places which hadn't seen me for thirty years.

After happily sharing in the conviviality of our preordained rendezvous as all six of us supped richly in an unpretentious restaurant which served the local white sausage and tasty gold mushrooms (grown, it had been darkly purported during my first visit to Lyons, in the dank basements of a city sprawled across twin arteries of water), I pleaded sudden fatigue and the need for my bed.

There was a flare of protest but it quickly died down as their social momentum jovially reasserted itself. I left to a chorus of fond goodbyes and 'See-you-in-the-mornings.'

I quickly put the genesis of succulent *ceps* right out of my head as the interred youth in the aging man guided me through the huddled lanes wedged between high blank walls on the west bank of the Saône.

Ignoring the funicular and climbing a myriad steps to enter the preposterous basilica of *Notre Dame de Fourvière* I noted that it was as campily grotesque as I'd remembered—even surpassing its ugly sister, the *Sacré Coeur* in Paris, which Ken and I visited from time to time when reliving the moribund glamour of Montmartre.

I didn't tarry there between 19th-century ill taste and the forlorn vestiges of Roman theaters from Lyons' Gallo-Roman past. Instead, I hurried down the steep slopes once more and buried myself amid the traboules and cramped alleys of the extensive sixteenth century portion of the city.

My motives for the abrupt descent weren't immediately clear to me. In fact the imprint of Lyons had, in a handful of hours, so filled my head with dreams and strange urgings that I would have been hard put to give rationalization to any of my actions save the most prosaic. I guess at the back of my mind there were the faintly exciting if unsavory recollections of the numerous erotic encounters the city had afforded my nineteen-year-old self—when every *pissoir* had been an invitation to sexual dalliance.

Dancing like ghosts within the tents of memory were men like the muscular blond who on hearing my English accent insisted on replying in broken German—confusing me with those gay members of the *Wehrmacht* who had retreated to the Fatherland nearly two years before the arrival of *Albion* in terms of one sex-starved student.

It was in a sense of *auld lang syne* that I entered a circular metal toilet, at the intersection of the medieval *rue des Vitriers* and the *rue des Plâtriers,* and recalled the presence of a large and stiff penis pointed proudly in my direction from the adjacent urinal.

I had fondled the smooth and jerking member with growing excitement on noting its owner was a dark-haired youth in cotton overalls who could have so easily been a wiry descendant of either the glaziers or plasterers after whom the two narrow streets had been named. But when he whispered a price, the glamour dissolved and I mentally said farewell to his cock as he slowly slid it back through the cotton slip and with constant inclinations of his head, invited me to follow him—presumably up one of the dark, sunless alleys of the *quartier.*

The first thing I noticed on this fresh visit was the total absence of graffiti—no *je veux sucer une grande bitte* with anatomically extravagant drawings as accompaniment to the invitation to fellatio. The rough slate face of the twin urinals had been replaced by shiny tin on which it was impossible to write.

The *pissoir* was also now not only more hygienic in its re-vamping but its aseptic air somehow suggested that it was no longer used as a gay rendezvous.

Such subtle changes were possibly the basis of my gradual modification of mood. I was still in a profoundly nostalgic frame of mind but on sauntering once more from the vacant urinal my thoughts turned to the other strand which had coloured my teenage pilgrimage to Lyons.

In 1947 I had resided some distance from Vieux Lyon where I now wandered. It had been in the house of a priest who ran a local radio station for the church and my experience there had been a little scary. Père Tourel had been hospitable enough but I soon sensed that he had scant patience for my schoolboy French and made no effort to accommodate my imperfect understanding.

The three days of my stay had signified some superb food—my first encounter with the delicious *ceps* mushrooms—and gratifyingly cheap accommodation which had been crucial to a student on an economy budget. But these advantages had been somewhat offset by oppressive periods of silence as when we sat at supper being served by a shuffling housekeeper who, by tight lips, had implied her resentment at my presence.

I often recalled the time at *Notre Dame des Ondes* when, in his tiny garden, I had desperately sought to alleviate the atmosphere by referring appreciatively to the wooden stations of the cross which dotted the gravel path we trod.

After much arduous preshaping of sentences in hopefully correct French I expressed my admiration at the beauty of their carving. Unfortunately I spoke of *Les Gares de la Croix* rather than *Les Stations.* L'Abbé Tourel was not amused, tersely corrected my error and asked sarcastically whether the pious devotion of the Stations of the Cross was practised as far north as rain-swept England. He'd then lapsed back into his customary laconicism.

However, the selfsame cleric was responsible for my having an extraordinary encounter and it was this I thought of now when again walking the criss-crossed alleys that had first lain under the humid, Lyonnais skies in the reign of Louis the Fourteenth.

One morning, after a brief breakfast—*café au lait* served in a huge ceramic cup and saucer, accompanied by the stale remnants of yesterday's stick of *pain maïs* which he softened by dunking—Père Tourel asked me whether I wished to accompany him to the Cathedral of St. Jean where he had business to conduct.

To this day I am grateful that I assented for it was in the gloom of that decrepit sandstone edifice, crumbling from ill-repair and with lumps of masonry littering the flagstones where they'd fallen from the tops of pillars and arches, that he introduced me to one of the most remarkable people I have ever met.

It was another priest. The Abbé Mercier was attached, it seemed, to the cathedral staff. His diminutive figure had instantly captivated me. In the first place, unlike my temporary landlord, this petit abbé was wearing a multi-buttoned, frayed soutane with clerical bands at his neck (which, with his lace-up boots, gave him a distinctly 19th-century appearance).

Even more memorable was his voice. In striking contrast to Père Tourel's mumbled drawl, this tiny priest spoke in both clearly enunciated French and in such measured tones I had no difficulty whatever in understanding his every word. I was even aware of his Lyonnais accent by the slightly pronounced syllables at the end of such words as *peut-être* and *Angleterre.*

On learning that I was an Anglican theological student he had at once suggested we leave the dust-festooned cathedral and repair to his rooms nearby. Père Tourel, I suspect, had been anticipating this for he explained to his colleague that he would now continue about his business at various ecclesiastical supply shops in the neighbourhood, collecting me at the Abbé's dwelling when he was done.

It was thus I entered the ordered rooms of the elderly priest and, while sitting on a hard chair facing him, experienced holiness.

It was this spiritual *fragrance,* if I can call it that, which I now quested on leaving the lavatory, some twenty years after I'd met what I suppose is the closest thing to a saint I am likely to meet.

I found the cathedral all right—that was hardly difficult. It was firmly bolted at that hour and in any case, I was not seeking to enter it. But for the life of me, after searching for the best part of an hour, I couldn't locate the flight of steep stone steps which had led to the Abbé Mercier's neat if minuscule apartment, set in the cathedral wall.

Perhaps there had been extensive alterations to the façade of the building since my visit all those years earlier. Perhaps memory was playing me tricks. I finally gave up the search, sat down on a stone plinth where centuries before a statue had been inserted, and laboriously resurrected my unexpected encounter with the slight elderly figure on that long ago Tuesday morning in 1948.

His white hairs had been cropped close to his skull. The smooth-shaven skin of his face was stretched tight and had a parchment-like pallor to it. That he wore dentures was obvious and his eyebrows were as white as the fringe above them. I was unable to remember whether he wore glasses though I have a notion he did wear a pair of cheap, wire spectacles.

That might have been the Abbé Tourel—or even both of them. If so there was little more I could recall that the two priests shared. Père Tourel might have been a bit of a dour cleric, unused to young men, particularly foreign ones who spoke poor French. But he was of normal clay and for me, at least, only distinctive and memorable for the role he briefly played in my youthful life.

The Abbé Mercier was of another cloth. Mortal, yes, but already straining to be free of this world. The physical sight of him isn't hard to delineate for his dress, as his mien, was simplicity itself. But from the second I saw him in the shadowy aisle of the cathedral to the long time we simply sat there facing each other as he asked me gentle questions about my upbringing and my future aspirations, I knew with eerie conviction he was not as other men.

His humility, his *emptiness* of self, seemed a vortex, sucking me away from self-concern, pulling me into reluctant flower from a hard bud of introspection. Under the calm of his compassion and the magnet of his abnegation I shed my fears, my tattered esteem and soiled hopes. Simply let him *love* me. He never for a moment threatened, or sought to bully his way into my hesitant places. I was not even tempted to confess sins, to reveal the taint of yesterday's sex that still hung as a stale aroma about my body. Nor was I minded to tell this tiny French priest with a high voice, of the awful dichotomies which threatened to rend me.

I spoke only in short words of my obdurate Catholic faith which I ardently hoped that he of *Ecclesia Gallica* and I of *Ecclesia Anglicana* shared. His eyes moistened in the intensity of his reply. He lifted his arms (whether in deliberate emulation of those suspended from the crucifix I have no means of knowing) and began to quote from memory.

I still recall every word—in the French he spoke:

Ce n'est pas seulement pour eux que je prie, mais encore pour tous ceux qui croiront en moi, en ajoutant foi à leur parole, afin que tous soient, comme vous, Père, vous êtes en moi, et moi en vous; afin qu'eux aussi soient en nous et que le monde croie que c'est vous qui m'avez envoyé.

His room was ill-lit and meager in furnishings. Yet at this point it seemed sacred in its stillness. The chair on which I'd sat for the best part of two hours was beginning to press cruelly against my bottom, but the discomfort of my flesh vanished in the intensity of his utterance of Jesus Christ's High Priestly Prayer. So achingly real was his identification with the divine yearning for unity, so much of his Master did he become before my wondering eyes, that I half expected him to stand up and turn from me as he followed Jesus, right after He'd uttered those words, over the brook Kidron to that awful garden of His betrayal.

Suddenly I felt my limbs being pulled apart—torn from their sockets in a flame of pain. I stared, transfixed, into the Abbé Mercier's face as the tears streamed down it. He was no longer quoting from St. John's Gospel but addressing me in a soothing flow of words.

"You are with him, too, my son. You know how He weeps from the rents which have torn in his Body the Church. Every day I say His prayer. Every day I feel His pain. We must learn to live His ache for our Unity."

"I am frightened, Father," I said. "I am hurting from things I don't understand."

"You will grow into them, my child. It is not for you yet. *Jésus, Je prie pour l'union*, this is the last agony."

His words, though so clear, so bell-like, were hardly more than a whisper. I doubt if anyone else could have heard him. His tone changed. I slowly recognized the Latin. I let myself slide from the hard chair to the carpetless floor to receive his forgiveness and blessing.

All that was what I now carefully resurrected in every detail as I sat there on that balmy spring night. I tried to join it to the intervening years—to the recent visit to the public john, to my relationship with Ken and with the two boys, those true *Sons of the Present,* who'd be with us for the rest of this memory-laden journey.

God, it was hard! It wasn't just the years between Père Mercier then and what we all stood for now. It wasn't even my egotistic *rue* with which I regarded what had happened to once disciplined, daily mass-attending me. There was also the obliterating notion that the scissors of selfishness in a whole generation had totally severed the Père Mercier past from our hedonistic present and apocalyptic future.

The Dodo was alive and well compared with that silly little sprite of a man in black drag who could get worked up to tears over a chimerical vision of ecumenical unity among a bunch of religious nuts who were, in any case, fast disappearing from the face of the earth.

I hurried in the direction of our hotel, anxious to be safely in bed and under the covers before the arrival of Ken. I suppose I was now most susceptible to anything he might say, knowing I'd not been acting particularly pleasantly since we'd arrived in France.

All of which was silly, really, for Ken was never flippant over my fluctuating moods, or judgmental over the perversity which had replaced the religious constancy which I had exhibited in our Parisian salad days.

I started making resolutions as I fled the *traboules* for the anodyne modernity of *L'Hôtel du Rhône.* As usual, they began with my relationship with my lover and my allowing him to love me in his own way. It moved from Ken to my two female friends and my tendency to encourage them to bitch one another.

There was the tired old hope that I'd attend Mass again regularly. Oddly enough, I only half-formulated an ambition to put myself out for both Derek and my godson. Yet in retrospect, it was there my resolve and strength were to prove most needed.

Alas, the spirit of little Father Mercier had been left far behind. Not that the city of Lyons provided any further intimations of past hope or present despair. Unlike Derek, Benjamin had gotten on famously with his French grandmother although there was a curious echo of my own experience with the linguistically inflexible Abbé Tourel from Jacqueline's father, a retired engineer who had returned to his native Lyons after many years in Algiers.

Monsieur d'Auligny had been inclined to treat his grandson as imbecilic because of his lack of fluency in his mother's tongue. Though I have to confess I was very proud of Benjamin's French as so superior to mine at a comparable age.

The connection, too, between the two visiting mothers with their thoroughly Canadian offspring and their grandparents was further compounded by absent fathers. In the case of Neil, he had for years been *persona non grata* with his in-laws for his insolence and disrespect.

In bringing us up to date over the visit, Jacqueline now added with pride in her voice for her son (but still with coldness for her spouse), how Benjamin had fiercely defended his Dad in a fiery display of Irish loyalty when his French hadn't for one moment failed him.

It wasn't surprising, then, that the next two days of sightseeing and shopping by the two women in the numerous chic boutiques of Lyons were punctuated by the incessant swopping of stories involving obtuse parents stuck in their parochial ways who were incapable of appreciating a younger generation—especially those from overseas and other cultures.

Fortunately, both Helen and Jacqueline exorcised the nattering from their systems and by the time we looked back for a last glimpse of ugly *Notre Dame de Fourvière* huddled atop the hill above *Vieux Lyon*, the six of us were chatting (in the perverse way of tourists with a common national background) of the place whence we'd come and of those left behind.

That didn't last too long. After lunch at *La Pyramide* in the nearby town of Vienne—over which the senior four rhapsodized as the finest lunch ever eaten—we all shared in planning our assault upon the *Côte d'Azur*. That was the region which Benjamin and Derek had chosen rather than an immediate westward sortie towards Perpignan. Ken and I had favoured the latter with a prior exploration of the Roman remains at Arles and Nîmes. But at least there was to be Avignon which we adults insisted would be ideal for our first night—over the pleas of the youngsters to drive straight down to the sea and its beaches.

Ken had turned in the first rental car and we now had an Impala which comfortably held the six of us as it quickly ate up the miles. From Lyons onwards a tentative sense of the south took on firmer characteristics across the countryside. The now ubiquitous presence of vines and the shape of bright red tiles, designed to contend with an aggressive sun, became more and more prominent and we saw our first clumps of mimosa and olive trees about farmhouse walls.

That first night together out of Lyons I made sure I remained allied to the group—a conscious desire to atone for my desertion on that earlier evening. But I couldn't suppress the revived memory of Abbé Mercier. It surfaced when I was walking alongside Derek on the banks of the Rhône at Avignon. We were trailing the others by a few meters and we had just passed a knot of French tourists, obviously enjoying the scents and sounds of late evening, with the battlements of the Palace of the Popes ghostly across the slow moving waters, under the stars.

"They're an ugly stunted lot, aren't they Uncle Davey?" the boy said conversationally. I would have corrected him anyway, hating that kind of lazy generalization as much as I did the avuncular title he sometimes accorded me.

But I tied my remonstrance to my experience of the little priest. "Not all the French are short," I said, "and some of the smallest are the most attractive."

He gave me a sharp look which even the dim light couldn't conceal. "I guess you'd know. Mum was saying in our hotel room that you've known this part of France from way back."

I'd never had a *tête à tête* with Derek about homosexual matters—but since a toddler he'd been present when we and his mother indulged uninhibitedly in camp chatter—with even Gordon sometimes participating, if grudgingly. An eavesdropper might well have concluded on some of our gin-and-tonic evenings at the Goddards' that we did little else than exchange gay gossip and make gay jokes. Certainly they were the occasions when the laughter was loudest and most hysterical.

I wasn't going to rupture established patterns under the skies of Provence! Or oblige him with spicy confessions of dalliance with dwarfs along that very river whose Avignon banks I'd known when I was also a youth, even if they'd occurred.

"I was referring to a priest I once knew. Back in Lyons. He was the most spiritual person I've ever met. He's naturally a lot on my mind considering we've just come from there."

Derek was eighteen—as I'd been reminded over our first dinner in Paris. He didn't prevaricate then—nor did he now. "You still go to church, don't you? It's something I don't know a whole lot about. Mum says I should read the Bible, the Koran and the Bhagavad-Gita before I decide for myself. I've looked at them but, Jesus, they're all so boring!"

"I'm not talking about books, however unreadable. I'm speaking of someone I once met in this part of the world. He was a Frenchman, a priest and well, he was *diminutive*, if you like."

"Did he try and convert you?"

"How could he? I was already converted."

"Did he know much about you?" I waited. I wasn't going to help him out. "I mean you just met him as a stranger—you were on vacation, right?"

"Right."

"So he really didn't know too much about you, did he?"

"Nor did he enquire. It wasn't an interrogation. We met in the main aisle of Lyons cathedral and then we went to his place for a chat while my host—another priest—shopped for charcoal, candles and incense—things like that. The kind of shops that sell church supplies are usually found in cathedral precincts."

"Is that so?" He didn't sound a bit interested. Not in ecclesiastical merchandise, that is. But he wasn't going to let go his first line of questioning, even so. "That was all before you'd ever met Uncle Ken, wasn't it?"

If I sounded tired it was because I'd heard that line of approach before, hundreds of times. "Yes, Derek, it was. But the point I was making was about a small man who gave off an incredible sense of power. Not that that's odd. Napoleon was a bit of a titch and so were lots of historical figures. But this man's power was his holiness. That's what was so unusual."

"Oh sure, now I see," the boy said. "It must've been something—to meet someone like that. I'd like to hear more about it but I think the others are waiting for us to catch up."

"Let's do that," I said crisply, welcoming the diversion. I knew then that it was highly unlikely I'd talk to Derek about the little priest again—let alone about holiness. The experience wasn't communicable between us, perhaps not between our generations. Perhaps with anyone at all.

"I'll race you to them," I said, starting to run but knowing he'd quickly overtake me and arrive first.

PART TWO

ELEVEN

≈

We made not for Nice but neighbouring Villefranche for our first night on the Mediterranean. This was in part due to the suggestion of both Jacqueline and Ken that the accommodations would be less expensive and that a fishing village would prove a more pleasant place to stay than the larger resort.

I had my own reason for backing them against Helen and the boys who argued for liveliness against what they feared was a sleepy backwater. Some years before, I had flown to Nice direct from London for a brief holiday with my Cousin, Loveday Yeo, and her physician husband, Timothy.

We had spent a blissful week exploring the coast from Nice eastwards to Monte Carlo and along to the Italian border at Menton. They owned a small yacht berthed in the port of Villefranche and I had delighted in the time spent sailing towards Torfino, first below the rugged Corniche and then along the *Costa dei Fiorc* of northern Italy.

I had given Ken glowing accounts of Villefranche (which reminded Loveday and me of the Cornish fishing villages of our childhood) and I was therefore anxious to share it all with him. I knew it was unlikely I'd ever return on my own as Timothy Yeo had died suddenly four years ago, from a car collision when visiting a farmer patient. His distraught widow now rarely left the moorland village of St. Breward where Tim had practised.

I had no difficulty in recalling directions as I drove directly to the Hotel Welcome on the quay in the center of town. It was sufficiently early in the summer season for us all to have adjoining rooms, nevertheless both Ken and I were quick to notice that there was at least one other male couple staying there and several other English-speaking families. I remembered that the hotel favoured British guests and that many of those renting sailboats and yachts booked rooms at the hotel for relief from cramped quarters below deck and the opportunity to relax with a hot bath or shower.

It was a warm enough evening for us to dine outside at the metal tables on the quay. Afterwards we split up. The boys and their mothers elected to walk the long length of the harbourfront with its series of bars and small fish restaurants while I hauled Ken off to show him where Tim and Loveday Yeo had rented their berth.

We passed three old men wearing berets and two youths in jeans and T-shirts, fishing with rods from the seawall, before taking the sharp curving causeway, bordered landward by stone ramparts towering high above us, away from the main part of Villefranche towards the yachting basin known locally as the *darse.*

"Dogshit lane, is what poor old Tim called this," I told Ken. "Better be careful where you walk." But in fact Ken was walking along the balustrade of the seawall staring out over the mouth of the harbour to where the squat lighthouse was beginning to flash in the gathering dusk.

The pungent smell of the Mediterranean tingled my nostrils and watered my eyes. I glimpsed a pair of linked lovers strolling about the gravel paths of the park above us and a few solitary figures hovering amid the clumps of palms. We could hear an incessant rattle from the marina long before we took the final curve around the headland and confronted the crowded *darse.* The source of the noise was the flapping of wire halyards atop metal masts—a modern marine sound which hadn't existed when Cousin Loveday and I had sailed our tiny sailboat with its rust-red Cornish rig down the broad estuary of the Camel. Then all had been wood and sisal ropes: fiberglass hulls unheard of.

I was hardly expecting to see Timothy Yeo's *Kernow* but I persuaded Ken to join me along the causeway to where she used to be anchored. Most of the vessels, jammed side by side like the proverbial sardines, were deserted—their owners either weekend sailors, or on shore dining at one of the numerous restaurants.

When we were almost at the end of the dock it was to find the new occupant of the Kernow's berth with a couple sitting on deck and the sound of further activity below in the lighted cabin. Music softly played and everything seemed extraordinarily peaceful in the approach of night.

What made me stop in my tracks were not these beguilements but the small shock of seeing a Canadian pennant, its blood red maple leaf vibrant in the cabin light, drooping from the stern. I barely had time to remark its presence to Ken when we were both addressed from the shadows riding the water.

"Hi, guys. Can we do anything for you?" The male voice was unmistakably North American; I assumed it was Canadian.

"We're just taking a stroll," I called back. And then, to explain our presence there on the dock: " My cousin used to berth his yacht where you have yours. It was the Kernow."

"So you must be related to the Yeos. Hey, Thelma, come on deck. There's relatives of Loveday and Tim up here." The voice's owner moved into the pool of light and we could now make out a burly man in white shirt and shorts. His curly hair was graying and he was wearing granny spectacles. I noticed a book in his hand.

"Come aboard the Gananoque, why don't you? It's good to meet friends of poor old Tim. He was a great guy and he's sure missed along the coast here."

When we had climbed the small gangplank and sat down in the cockpit and exchanged names with Dennis Willnough and his wife, Thelma, I explained in further detail why we'd stopped by the Gananoque.

"We saw the Canadian flag. We're from Vancouver ourselves, you see."

Dennis threw us a glance which I felt had nothing to do with where we were from. "You just taking a vacation together, then?"

Ken took over. "In fact there are six of us. There're also two women with teenaged sons. But they took a walk along the quay while Davey wanted to see the *darse* again to show me where his cousin's boat had been berthed."

"Can I get you something to drink?" Thelma enquired. "We must celebrate *Hockey Night in Canada* or something. Dennis and I are from Kingston. He teaches at Queens."

That led naturally to the information that Ken was a prof at UBC and in return we learned that the husband was an anthropologist and that the Willnoughs, Halegonians both, had been coming down to Villefranche for nearly twenty years. We also gathered that they had one child, a fifteen-year-old daughter who, after a day's sailing with friends on a neighbouring boat, was at that moment sleeping soundly up in the Gananoque's fo'c'sle.

It was soon apparent that the Woolnoughs were distinctly old-fashioned in their marital structure. No hint of women's liberation disturbed the beck-and-call role that Thelma played. It was she who bobbed below deck again to procure the drinks we selected and then again for more ice from the ship's tiny refrigerator. Again, it was she who, at the jerk of his head or wave of his hand, dove for a second and third bottle of the wine he'd offered. It was she who opened canisters and cartons to provide pâté, biscuits and several varieties of cheese for us to munch along with the *pétillant* bottles of rosé which, Dennis unnecessarily informed us, was the *vin du pays* of the Midi.

The talk was far-ranging. As fellow-Canadians, we naturally covered the cosmic conspiracy to ignore our country and passed from that to a shared conviction the world was currently run by lawyers and thus en route to hell in a handbag!

We somehow also managed to embrace the problems of western separatism from a B.C. viewpoint, the deficiencies of *la nouvelle cuisine*, the vulgarity of Richard Nixon, and the problems of child-rearing—with our bachelor comments conveniently drawn from the experiences of our friends and their teenage offspring.

Dennis Woolnough started to expound on the sexual disposition of their fifteen-year-old daughter, Muriel. "Keep your voices down because the kid sleeps lightly. But I tell you it worries me when she goes out with Henri and Hugette in that goddamn skiff of theirs. She always comes back dead tired and won't speak about the day they've spent. Thelma refuses to admit it but Muriel looks haggard and pale when a day in the sun and wind should have the opposite effect.

"If you ask me that bloody *Monégasque* is itching to get his fingers down her pants. I've seen the looks between them and it isn't just that between a forty-year-old man and the kid daughter of his friend."

"Oh come *on*, Dennis! Let's not have all that nonsense again." Thelma looked distinctly unhappy as she turned to us. "That's one of his favourite topics when he's had too much to drink. It's just his paranoia talking."

Ken sought to maneuvre the talk away from a topic which was patently embarrassing our hostess. "Well, she wouldn't keep going sailing with them if it was making her unhappy. I sure hated going out on the water when I was a kid."

"I never said she didn't *like* it, my friend. That's the problem. I'm afraid I have a daughter who's all too keen to share what she's got between her legs. What do you think of a little girl one morning displaying her treasure to every evil-minded brat down here on the *darse*?"

Thelma exploded. "The child was nine and she was showing her *mosquito* bite, for God's sake! Won't you ever let that drop? Let's get off the bloody subject for once." Her voice changed abruptly. "I say, how about you getting your gang to come over tomorrow and we can have a picnic and a sail out there in Villefranche Bay. Do you think they'd like that?"

It wasn't hard to perceive her plea—however soft her tone and however shaded her eyes from the pool of the light in the yacht's cockpit. Ken looked at me and I got the message.

"I think they'd love it—if it's okay with the two of you. But don't change your plans just because of this chance encounter."

Dennis looked dully at his empty glass. "We don't have any plans. The kid goes off and we just laze around. It will be good for her to stay with her family and good for us to have a bit of focus for a change. Anyway, Thelma is dying for a bit of female company. I think it a great idea! Let's have a drink on it. Fetch up more rosé, Mother!"

This time Ken and I anticipated one another. "It's time we headed back," we chorused. "Thanks all the same," I added. "Especially if you want the crowd of us here by a reasonable time. Two women take long enough but two male teenagers seem to take just as long—don't they, Ken?"

My companion agreed as he stood up to join me. "What time do you suggest?" he asked Thelma. "Around noon?"

But Thelma's spark—possibly born of opposition to her husband—appeared to have lapsed again. "When do you say, darling?"

Dennis Woolnough still sat, glass in hand. He tugged angrily at his beard but whether from the lack of *vin rosé* or in frustration at our impending departure it was hard to tell. "You'd better make it eleven so that we can split the main-brace at a decent hour. That'll give us some real sail time too and we can get far enough away from all the pleasure craft that block the harbour roads."

I had the feeling he was still burning because his will had been thwarted and we weren't staying to drink with him deep into the night. I said as much as we left them on deck. Two isolated figures, one sitting, one standing. She waved vigorously until we'd actually left the floating duckboards of the dock.

"I really liked her," I commented. "I'm not so sure about him."

"There's much more to him than we got tonight," Ken answered as we set off round the causeway towards the fishing port. "I don't think he really liked us but we piqued his interest."

I laughed. "It won't be the first time that's happened, will it? On the other hand, I thought she was relaxed right from the start. Then women usually are."

"Don't generalize too early," Ken warned. "By this time tomorrow night your opinions might have turned completely around."

I was pondering that when we had our final adventure of the day. Perhaps *incident* would better describe what happened as we arrived at the last curve of 'dogshit lane' and the lights of Villefranche hove into sight.

The high walls of the medieval ramparts to our left had given way to the park where, on our way to the *darse*, we had seen figures flitting. It was too dark to see anyone between the bushes and palms now, but suddenly we heard the sound of running, what could have been a police whistle, and hoarse shouts. At any moment I expected someone to come running down to the path we were on but that didn't happen. The patter of feet on gravel grew fainter and the whistle didn't sound again.

Uncharacteristically, neither of us commented on the incident but stayed with the topic of the Woolnoughs and tomorrow's prospect of a pleasant sail with some compatriots.

I did decide, though, to discreetly investigate the park above us while we stayed in Villefranche. Although on my previous visits to Cousin Loveday I hadn't come across any gay rendezvous I had strongly suspected the existence of one. The desperate sound of fleeing steps and my belief that we had just heard the law in pursuit, convinced me I now knew precisely where.

The promise of the following morning proved all that any local *Syndicat d'initiative* could have hoped for. By the time we were finally assembled for breakfast on the terrace, the cloudless sky contained a comfortably warm sun while across the road the Mediterranean dazzled in an intensity that made the term *Côte d'Azur* almost an understatement.

It probably helped explain the blithe mood which had settled over our sextet but I suspected it was also abetted by the boys' instinctive satisfaction over the fact we would be staying in one place for a little while. Then the young—this trip was already suggesting—were more conservative than their elders in confronting novel experience.

In any case, the two mothers and we bachelor uncles were more disposed to align our moods to those of the boys and to compromise in the cause of group unity. I am quite sure, though, that neither Benjamin nor Derek were, for a moment, aware of such concessions.

A huge pile of croissants arrived. The bearer was a comely young man in a horizontally striped T-shirt and skin tight navy blue pants. I glanced quickly at Ken. Helen glanced quickly at me. Jacqueline laughed out loud. Her son's glance raked the lot of us and his face clouded. In distinctly accented but grammatical French he told the waiter he personally wanted a brioche and not the croissant.

"The croissant come with the *petit déjeuner*, m'sieur. It is included with your room charge." He smiled at Benjamin, revealing white teeth. "Beside, we don't have no brioche at the Welcome."

He looked at the rest of us as he stood between Ken and Jacqueline, his legs slightly parted. I could've sworn he wasn't wearing underpants.

. . .

My godson was both unimpressed and certainly unabashed. "Then bring me some bread," he ordered. "I guess the Welcome at least has that."

"Of course, m'sieur. I will fetch it at once." But he didn't move right away. He remained there—lewdly displaying his masculinity as he smiled at each in turn. "The croissant are to your liking?"

We all assented. Derek had already split his apart and was heaping it with butter and black-cherry jam. As the waiter left Jacqueline raised an eyebrow. "I don't think he makes his living just from tips."

"Nor would I if I looked like him," Helen added drily. Benjamin's scowl deepened, if that were possible, but he said nothing. Derek devoured a huge chunk of jam-dripping croissant. Uncle Ken obviously decided the moment propitious for bringing up the invitation from the Woolnoughs to spend the day sailing on their boat.

The reply was both instant and positive from the lads, with Benjamin obviously welcoming the distraction. This time it was his mother who appeared cautious and prepared to be at variance from the majority.

Her eyes narrowed as she stared out beyond the still waters of the harbour. "The weather looks perfect but I know this Mediterranean. If there's any chance of it changing I think I'll stay here. I wouldn't want to ruin it for everyone else."

"Derek, too, can be a lousy sailor," his mother put in. "In spite of anything he may say now, I've had him retching on the ferry to Nanaimo when there was only a bit of a swell."

"That's a crock, Mum!" her son mumbled between mouthfuls. "I'd had the 'flu' and you said yourself we should've taken the seaplane."

"I wouldn't worry either of you," Ken said pacifically. "Dennis has a ship-to-shore telephone and his wife told us she's a terrible sailor. She makes him regularly call the *Météo* in Nice to see if there's any chance of it being what she calls *agitée*. Besides, they have a teenaged daughter and I gather from Thelma that she's most fussy about the weather—even if she does go sailing as much as possible with friends of theirs in the *darse*."

That seemed to pacify both women—at least they agreed with the general proposal—provided there was no change in the weather before it was time to cast off. Benjamin's rather truculent mood with the slim-waisted waiter seemed to have dissipated. Due in part, perhaps, to the appearance of the bread rolls, but also, I suspected, from the reference to the Woolnoughs' teenaged daughter.

"Who was that kid you mentioned who'd be on board? Someone's daughter, you say?"

"*Everyone* is someone's daughter—or son," Derek said sarcastically. "They said the Woolnoughs. You going deaf or something?"

The look Benjamin offered him was possibly darker than that he'd vouchsafed the amply endowed waiter.

Later that morning, though, after meeting the Woolnoughs, and we'd all settled either in the cockpit or along the deck of the Gananoque, somewhat different patterns established themselves than I'd anticipated. It was Derek who sat with Muriel at the prow of the ship as it rode rhythmically up and down through the sun-shot water. (So much for his mother's fears of seasickness for her son considering he'd chosen the place on board where most movement was to be experienced!)

Benjamin had elected to join us men in the cockpit where Dennis captained the vessel, one hand loosely on the tiller, a glass of rosé in the other. All three mothers were spread-eagled on the warm fiberglass of the deck, soaking up the sun in pursuit of tans. Derek and Muriel, a blonde and busty girl looking distinctly mature for her years, were in animated conversation from the moment they moved forward out of earshot.

The women were virtually silent although there were spasmodic remarks from Thelma as she vainly sought to engage an unusually quiet Helen in conversation. With us four males it was quite different. Although Benjamin usually addressed me, his contributions were patently intended for the others, too. There was a lot of talk about sailing, with a heavy sprinkling of nautical jargon from our skipper. At one point I noticed him throw an enquiring glance towards the two kids now standing above where the Gananoques's bows cut through the water.

"Why don't you give Derek a spell?" I murmured to Benjamin, "and have a chat with Muriel yourself."

Dennis overheard and shook his head. "Let them enjoy each other. It isn't like her being out here with that Henri Sartori. At least she's with someone her own age."

For a moment I feared Ken might pedantically point out the difference in years between them but he refrained and I immediately felt guilty for prejudging him.

"Do you ever swim from over the side, Mr. Woolnough?" Benjamin asked. I had noticed that both he and Derek had shed their jeans on climbing aboard and were now wearing only swim shorts. It was obviously something they'd contemplated.

"I don't, but there's no earthly reason why not. That is if you guys are good swimmers. It's no place for beginners. And call me Dennis, for God's sake. My own daughter does!"

I didn't interrupt but I was pretty sure that both Benjamin and Derek would call Dennis 'Uncle' rather than by his Christian name.

Ken and I had discussed it with them and they both preferred to confine first name usage to their friends and peers. The subject didn't come up because Dennis at once slackened the throttle and the Gananoque slowed perceptibly.

"Good thing we didn't run up the mainsail and jib right away," he grunted, pulling hard on the tiller so that we came around. "It's much easier for diving off and climbing on again when we aren't under sail."

Thelma sat up. "You've given him a perfect excuse, Benjamin," she said, grinning. "He'll do anything to avoid putting those sails up—especially when he has to rely on his two ham-fisted women. This way he can use the engine all day and he prefers that. You're looking at someone who'd love to be a professional yachtsman but hates the hard work that goes with it."

I was surprised he didn't contradict her. Then he seemed altogether more relaxed out there than in the darse the previous evening. His blue eyes under bushy eyebrows squinted as his craft rode the waves under the sunny immensity of sky. He had grown more distant, acted as if he were alone on the Gananoque as it shuddered in response to his firm hand at the tiller.

After a sumptuous lunch, which included several pâtés and cheeses from the local grocery store, Dennis put the instruments on automatic, posted both boys and his daughter as lookouts and declared he was for what he called a 'zizz.'

Considering what I had seen him steadily put away since we'd first set sail, I wasn't surprised. Then I think we'd all drunk enough (including a remarkable '47 Beaune which had materialized with the lunch) to appreciate a nap ourselves.

I found the same section of deck where Thelma had lain that morning and in spite of the discomfort from halyards and hawsers closed my eyes. My body may have encountered a little difficulty with neatly coiled ropes, and resistant cleats and stanchions, but my head brimmed with comforting thoughts. Just before I'd lain down I'd noticed all three youngsters huddled in the bow and chatting away like magpies. Obviously they were getting on famously. Similarly, I decided, our two women had taken to Thelma for they had all gone below decks to use the heads and tidy up the tiny galley after the meal.

Ken and Dennis were stretched out on the benches around the cockpit, lying on their backs and staring up into the blue as they made desultory talk. It occurred to me that here I was gliding smoothly through those cobalt waters where people around the globe would give eye-teeth to be. Probably at that very moment as I started to drift off, there were film stars, famous statesmen, millionaire businessmen, out there with us off the French coast, enjoying the clichéd lifestyle of the Mediterranean.

The notion of trespass on the domains of privilege brought enormous satisfaction and certainly fed my Celtic sense of impudence in experiencing such luxury, purely by chance encounter. So we weren't exactly sailing on a luxury yacht owned by an Onassis but it was surely some step up from the first-cousin-to-a-lobster-boat I'd known in my Cornish childhood.

It was the sweet satisfaction of all that, I think, which finally bore me off.

TWELVE

≈

For a moment I thought I was the only one awake. Through the slits of my eyes I counted three heads. Their youthful owners, Derek and Muriel on one side of the prow, Benjamin on the other, were sitting with bare legs straddling the sides so that their feet were washed by the spray from the bows.

From the opposite direction I heard Dennis Woolnough's voice. Craning my neck I could see it was Jacqueline he was speaking to. That didn't surprise me. Men often found her a good listener—at least a more *sympathique* one than brusquely British Helen, who rarely went out of her way to be encouraging to males.

I moved a fraction closer to them and shut my eyes again. There are few things I enjoy more than eavesdropping.

"Each year we find it harder to go back. It's not just the job—though that's dull enough. It's squeaky-clean Kingston which suffocates. Although it's half way between Montreal and Toronto, it's only 'The Big T' that counts. Everything's at the mercy of 'Toronna'—which tries so hard to play second fiddle to New York. There's the real problem. Everything's *second*—second-rate and second-hand. It all happened some place else—not to mention some time before. No wonder Canada's spelt with a yawn!"

"No one lives in our country for the excitement," Jacqueline observed. "The secret is to have enough positive energy in yourself and what you're personally doing. That's how we survive in Vancouver, anyway. Davey says Vancouver is not so much laid back, as people claim, but laid *out*!"

There was a brief silence. I thought I could hear movement from below. "I guess what I'm really saying is that I'm fed up with teaching anthropology. I no longer respect my colleagues."

"Perhaps you need a change of location. Been too long in one place."

I could almost hear a shrug in Dennis' voice. "Where would I go? Neither of us ever want to see Halifax again. And out where you are—well, that's just too far for a couple of Maritimers. I do as little as

I can in the Department or for the University. I doubt if there's anywhere else now that would want me!" The whine was something I hadn't heard before.

"You can never really know those things," Jacqueline objected. "My husband always talks like that and I know perfectly well he's really admired by lots of his colleagues."

I grinned to myself. It was a pleasure to hear her lying through her teeth on behalf of the man she claimed to detest so much. Dennis wasn't interested in her solace.

"It doesn't really matter. Thank God I can get over here to France where there's enough work to make me forget all that campus crap."

"You're lucky to have this boat and to like sailing. I gather it's very absorbing."

"I didn't mean the Gananoque. Mercifully there's other things to blot out Queens and its shitty anthropology department."

"Oh, Dennis! You like the Ferrises—at least Beverly. And what about your old drinking buddy. Doesn't Ted MacDonald count any more?"

Thelma's voice now joined the fray. For a while she seemed to take over. "Dennis suffers from what I call the ocean blues when he's at sea. Pity is he gets them too rarely as we don't leave the harbour that often! But don't think that it's entirely gloom and doom back home on Bagot Street, Jacqueline. It's simply that Dennis always exaggerates. Because he so enjoys the long vacations he feels he has to hate the corresponding term-time."

I got the impression Thelma was making a distinct attempt to change the conversation. If so, Helen, who had also now surfaced from the cabin, subconsciously helped her.

"My God, what luxury problems you people have! My old man wouldn't know what a long vacation was if it hit him! They don't go in for such things at the phone company. In any case, he's such a patsy he's only really happy when he's being exploited. Which isn't surprising considering that being screwed is a way of life with my Gordon!"

I almost bit my tongue. Helen liked to be daring with her remarks but that was even further than she was prone to go!

It was time, I felt, I announced my own awakened presence. "Hi, everyone! Is that Corsica on the starboard bow?"

Our captain replied. "That's the portside, landlubber! And if that's Corsica we should hit Malta by nightfall! As a matter of fact it's somewhere near Beaulieu and we should be back in Villefranche within the hour."

I felt a general distress aboard the Gananoque at the thought our voyage would soon be over. When I stood up and looked towards the three young people I was convinced there'd be at least two in melancholy spirits when we finally berthed. Derek and Muriel were looking at each other with that peculiar intensity which animates adolescents in love. At that moment, though, the immediate future was hidden for them as they stared into each other's eyes while the vessel sprayed its way through the hitherto unbroken surface of the sea.

Benjamin, denied their mutual electricity, saw me, waved, and made his way aft, scowling.

"I see Derek's made a friend," I commented, wanting the pain of his exclusion out in the open and suspecting he was loathe to allude to it. "It always happens so quickly and seems so powerful. Someone really should do a study on shipboard romances."

"She's a flirt," Ben said savagely. Then looked me in the eye. "He didn't have a chance. She may be only fifteen but that's sure not the way she acts. If you ask me, she's an old hand at shipboard romances—if that's what you wanna call 'em!"

"You'd better not suggest that to her father," I told him. "Then there really *would* be an explosion. He's already convinced she's been seduced by one of his yachting friends. At least over Derek he can't accuse either of them of that."

"I don't like him any more than his daughter," my frank young friend informed me. "He's pissed all the time and when you were asleep he was really slobbering over Mum."

"Benjamin, you have the makings of a repulsive puritan. Next thing you'll be complaining about your Aunt Helen smoking and then perhaps you'll decide to tell me what rubs you particularly the wrong way about myself."

I tried to sound casual but in fact I was picking my words with great deliberation. I was near territory germane to Ken and me which I knew Benjamin would die rather than articulate. Yet this penchant for facile judgements of people on the part of the sixteen-year-old—something I'd never noticed back home in Vancouver—truly riled me.

I suspected, of course, that we were only a hair's-breadth from a condemnation of his father with all these judgments flying about. And I was as determined to defend Neil, if needs be, as I was keen to have my handsome godson instinct with generosity over the motives of others.

He grimaced. "Sorry," he said. "I didn't mean it that way. I've always told you what popped into my head, that's all."

If we hadn't been standing there mid-deck, a cynosure for all, I would have hugged the boy to me for his spontaneous intimacy.

As it was I just threw him a light punch to the arm. "Asshole," I said. "I wouldn't want you to ever act any other way—or I'd not speak to you again. Now let's join the oldies and we'll be a team playing at being sociable for the last little while, 'til we hit port, eh?"

When I put it that way, I had absolute confidence he'd do just that.

THIRTEEN

≈

When we trooped off the Gananoque—to the protestations of the hospitable Woolnoughs that we should stay on board for supper at the mooring in the darse—I knew that at least one of us would be returning very soon. It was obvious that Muriel wanted to accompany Derek and have dinner with us but her father had ruled otherwise—suggesting, as compromise, that we picnic in the hills behind Villefranche the very next day.

Although that idea hadn't been rejected before we clambered down the gangplank, as a result of a family council over dinner at another of the quay restaurants, it was decided (Derek voting contrary but without fuss) that we spend the next day sight-seeing in the vicinity. So the following morning was taken up with visiting Monte Carlo (chosen by the boys), Beaulieu, Juan les Pins, and Cap Antibes.

With the aid of a couple of guidebooks we were able to drive at least up to the gates of the Riviera homes of such historic figures as Winston Churchill and Lord Beaverbrook. The list also included the residences of movie stars like David Niven, and Errol Flynn (whose legally embroiled vessel, the stripped-down Zacca, the Woolnoughs had pointed out when we'd sailed back into the *darse* at Villefranche).

But these so singularly 20th-century dead—as we glimpsed their erstwhile monied façades behind screens of cypress and tall, wrought-iron gates—actually seemed more remote than characters from our century's fiction. With the exception of Somerset Maugham at his *Villa Mauresque*—who would represent for Ken and me the era's emblem of the tormented, self-hating queen—the others paled against the likes of the indomitable Blanche Dubois, Thomas Mann's Tadzio, Joyce Carey's ebullient artist Gully Jimson, or the doomed Sebastian of *Brideshead Revisited.*

I was mentally adding candidates along these lines as we drove the winding roads between the discreet residences of the rich when I was startled to hear Ken say that none of these public personages would burn so brightly for those of the century creeping up on us as the characters liberated in fiction and drama.

He, too, mentioned Blanche before going on to suggest the Joad Family of *The Grapes of Wrath* and Francois Mauriac's *Thérèse.*

"My God!" I exclaimed. "I was just thinking exactly the same thing! It's another example of ESP."

"It isn't, you know," Helen bluntly disagreed. "It's just one more example of close couples growing more and more mentally alike."

"I'll buy that," I said, as we descended towards the beach at Cap Ferrat where Derek and Benjamin wanted to swim. "But it can be quite eerie, you know—especially when it's something Ken and I've never even discussed before."

I knew whom my godson was addressing, although he offered no name and was staring away from me, out of the car window. "What's people living together got to do with it? Have you forgotten a little thing called *coincidence*?"

Ken took up the thread, agreeing that coincidence was far too underrated nowadays. He added professorially that it was probably an over-reaction to the likes of Dickens and the Victorian novelists.

I couldn't rid my mind of the notion that Benjamin was troubled more by Helen's direct allusion to Ken and me than to *synchronicity.* A general evacuation from the crowded automobile prevented my pressing the matter. Lying contentedly on the trucked-in sand (to offset the indigenous pebbles) the subject was temporarily dropped.

It was obvious long before we had sunbathed, and swum in the warm water, that the youngest member of our party could hardly constrain himself in a desire to see the nubile Muriel again. It was not his mother but Jacqueline who abetted him to the extent of suggesting that she, too, would like to return early to the hotel—to select postcards from the adjacent *tabac* and write them before doing anything else.

By late afternoon our party had disintegrated as its components went their several ways. I know that Derek was once more with Muriel because they were silhouetted against the dying sun on the Gananoque while Ken and I sat once more with Dennis drinking cocktails while his wife busied herself below decks in preparing supper for all six of us.

Our two women had taken the car into Nice where they intended shopping before taking drinks at the bar of the Négresco Hotel—to relive, they said, Edwardian times for potent absinthe concoctions. On mentioning this to Dennis he at once offered us a pernod or a Ricard but we declined. We both had a suspicion we were still several drinks away from dinner and what with wine during the meal and scotch or liqueurs after it, we let prudence guide us with a deliberate pacing of what we imbibed.

As it was, by the time we'd devoured Thelma's *veau à la crème* to the accompaniment of three bottles of *Midi vin rosé*, the lights from the various causeways around the *darse* were blurred to my eyes and I felt very blithe in spirit.

Although Thelma joined us after supper, when the two youngsters laughingly occupied themselves with the washing up, she made little contribution to the general discussion which was once more dominated by Dennis' opinions vis-a-vis the Common Market.

Ken and I had sobered up within an hour or so of dinner and with sobriety came the realization that I was more than a little bored. I was about to suggest it was time to return down dogshit lane when Ken, forestalling me, rose saying he'd now make his way back to the Welcome with Derek and Muriel who were anxious for a walk under the stars.

I was about to stand up, too, when Dennis grabbed my arm and begged me to stay for a nightcap. He promised he would then accompany me in order to escort his daughter on her return.

It is on such occasions I am always weakest. I chided myself for total lack of will, even as I sagged back and agreed to the request. Though I did silently curse the back of my lover as the three of them shouted farewells and disappeared into the darkness.

If I had been half-expecting to share the onus of listening to Dennis with his wife I was to be quickly disappointed. Within a quarter of an hour—I looked at my watch—she made her excuses to retire below, pleading there was much tidying up before she could flop on her bunk in the cramped bow compartment.

I sighed to an impervious Dennis, swirled my grotesquely large cointreau in its brandy snifter, and settled to the task of half-listening while I watched the dim shapes of fast-moving clouds overhead.

I don't know how long I sat there—or even how many cointreaus I consumed—before I grew aware that there was a shift in my host's mood and a decided change to his conversation. He had moved opposite me, bringing his head so conspiratorially close to mine that I knew first a flare of embarrassment and then one of alarm. Was he going to kiss me? Osculation—to which at least I was used with other men—soon proved to be the least of my worries!

"Good, I think she's turned in," he began. "An opportunity like this doesn't happen often. I feel I must use it to tell you a few things about myself I have never told another soul."

I looked away from the heavens—down at the swirling black water lapping below. If he wasn't going to make a pass, I was going to have the kind of late night confession that so many of us gays have experienced—those which are carefully obliterated from memory the next day by the trite excuse of having had too much to drink.

"Not a day goes by when my life isn't threatened, Davey. I'm quite likely to be shot on sight if certain people knew my identity or what the Gananoque is all about."

Racing skies and heaving waters were forgotten. I put down my snifter and stared at him. He had my attention now all right! In the cockpit light I searched his face—still just a few inches from my own. His blue eyes gleamed with a fierceness I couldn't fathom. His rather podgy and by no means steady hand tossed down his cognac as if it were water.

"I'm CIA, you see. The drug trade is my specialty, with the Middle East and North African traffic my present assignment."

"I thought that came under INTERPOL or something of the sort."

"So it does, I guess. But when it comes to drugs paying for arms and arms destined for terrorists it's very much *our* ballgame."

I sat silent. Watching him. I didn't even blink. He went on more quickly. "My job's rather different from the way these things appear on TV and the movies. I'm here simply to watch. To keep my eyes and ears open for every little whisper about suspected arrivals and pick-ups. You may know that from Nice to Marseilles is the drug gateway to Europe and eventually North America?"

My westcoast patriotism was flicked. "I thought that Vancouver was a major entry point for Canada and the U.S."

"Have you heard of the French Connection?"

"I even saw the movie," I told him with a smile. But anything even remotely to do with humour was definitely not on Dennis' agenda.

"I sometimes worry about Thelma and the kid. *They* wouldn't hesitate to grab them and even torture them to get what they wanted from me. I've asked for them to be left in Kingston but it was no-go from above. They're needed as a cover for both me and the Gananoque which is just about to be re-outfitted with all the latest hardware. It's that which worries me and is why I'm letting you in on all this."

I scanned his face, striving for clues, but his expression was rigid in sincerity. Aghast, I let him continue—without question or comment.

"What I'm getting to is this. I'm empowered to *recruit*, you see. What I thought—well, the two of you. I mean, two *guys* . . . no one would suspect, you see. Don't get me wrong. It's not that you're *obvious* or anything like that."

But I needn't have worried. In the next breath he relieved me of my worst fears. "I can't promise you riches, exactly. At least not right away. But I might as well tell you while we're being frank with each other that I am about to rather radically change my life style. I haven't dared mention it to Thelma yet but when a certain old man dies in Rome I shall be inheriting millions! How about that?"

His hands were trembling so violently now, the ice in his glass rattled like castanets.

"Congratulations," I piped up, as I felt an immense load slipping away.

He seemed unaware of anything I did or said. "Name of Smith mean anything to you?"

"No more than Jones."

That was the only time he threw me an odd look.

"No? Then why the hell should you know anything about the last of the Stuarts?"

"Why should I, indeed! In fact the only thing I think I know at the moment is that it's late and I am very tired. I really must go." I looked around for a place to put my glass.

He stirred in alarm. "No! Don't go." Only it wasn't so much a request as a command. "It's another reason I have to be in France, you see. It's not so much the title—that means nothing to me at all. But the Stuart money—and my ancestors were smuggled to Cape Breton with the peasants after The Highland Clearances—it's all sitting at St. Germain-en-Laye since 1788. Did you know that my full name is Charles Edward Louis Philip Casimir and that the Stuart was dropped and changed for Woolnough to put those damned Hanoverians off the scent?"

"No, I didn't know that. I guess I'm not much up on family trees. Or Legitimists versus Pretenders come to that."

I might have saved my breath.

"What I know you don't fucking know, Mister—Mister—"

"Bryant," I supplied amiably.

"—is that there are millions and millions of dollars involved. Probably the largest fortune in the eighteenth century. And in gold, my young friend. In gold there in St. goddamn Germain where he lived so long."

"I really must go." This time I did stand up.

"It won't all go to the CIA I can tell you that. Though I shall certainly see that my wife and child get the protection they deserve. I should also see that you two fruits—I'm sorry—that just slipped out. You two *fellas* get properly paid."

"I should say goodbye. It's been a *marvelous* evening."

"Most of it though will go to the Institute for World Government of which I shall be First President. We shall start by arraigning bastards like Idi Amin and all dictators and tyrants who can't be got by due process. We shall kidnap them and try them before the new World Tribunal. So you're looking at a totally new world justice system."

"Don't bother to see me off. I know that gangplank by now!"

"To kidnap those bastards we shall have a special corps fitted with a personalized shoulder-pack rocket system I've invented."

"Nighty-night then. See you in the morning probably" (vowing I wouldn't!).

On the cool night air I could still hear his progressively hoarse voice as I hastened up the springy causeway between the moored vessels.

"The arms are here, the sites chosen and the uniforms are due any day. I'll see that you—you—Ah, you *stupid* sonofabitch! I'm wasting my fucking time! You can't even hold your drink like a fucking man!"

I stopped when on firm ground and strained my ears. His shouts were no longer intelligible. But I could still hear his voice—along with that of an hysterical Thelma. As I turned the elbow along dogshit lane I thought I could also hear crying. But that could've been my imagination.

FOURTEEN

≈

I didn't tell Ken when I returned what had happened on the Gananoque. I didn't tell any of them. My motives were very diverse. I'm sure other minorities have similar experiences, but when I'm confronted with homophobia one response is personal *guilt*—so that I have to summon up emotional steam to be able to tell another gay. Yes, even Ken.

There was embarrassment over Woolnough, too. Perhaps shame. Mere drunkenness I could've coped with. Alcoholism was harder. The dementia surfacing as crazy illusion (whether over spying, kinship to the famous or the expectation of millions!) was something I needed space to absorb— let alone discuss with others.

I suspect that I have also toyed so excessively with fantasy that, observing it in Dennis Woolnough, it appeared as a personal warning. I do know that before I went to sleep next to a faintly snoring Ken, I solemnly swore off dreams of *Davey Bryant, Superman: Putting the World's Ills to Right*, as too uncomfortably close to the mad imaginings of poor Dennis ranting his hallucinations under the stars.

The next morning I made only cursory allusion to the event by stating publicly at breakfast that Dennis had been pissed again and that I thought I'd detected the preamble to a major row with Thelma before I had passed from earshot. As postscript I added that I thought he was perilously close to the DT's. I didn't elaborate.

The women were poring over our Michelin of the Marseilles area, Benjamin was arguing with Ken why different coloured wines predominated in one area over another. Only Derek proffered me his full attention.

"I hope Muriel didn't get dragged into it. When he's like that he hits her, you know. He's so damn jealous. Maybe I should slip over there. She says he goes on at her as if he were a lover or something."

I was not about to follow *that* up. "The state he was in I'd be very surprised if he sees the light of day before noon. I gather her mother tends to sleep in, too. You'd better let sleeping dogs lie, old man. In any case, I don't think you'd be very popular aboard the Gananoque this morning."

The boy made no comment but by the compressed mouth I suspected my advice was neither appreciated nor about to be taken.

I wasn't going to let adolescent romance play havoc with my intentions. I was still smarting from the general indifference to my announcement — feeling that somehow all of them were cheapening or diluting Dennis' disturbing revelations of insanity—even if I hadn't revealed to them precisely what I'd been through.

"We should leave for Nice and make sure we keep out of his hair for the rest of our time. I can assure you all that Dennis Woolnough in that state is *not* an attractive experience."

Jacqueline finally did meet my eyes. I think she knew I was holding things back but as she roved the table I sensed she also knew this was neither the time nor place for amplification.

"That's okay with me. We were just discussing where we should go next. The boys haven't seen anything of Nice and although it's only next door I reckon it's worth twenty-four hours. Besides, this hotel is rather unsatisfactory."

I could just imagine who told her that. Beware of mothers acting as their offspring's sounding board! So Benjamin had neither forgotten nor forgiven the swishy young waiter we'd had on the first day. I smiled to myself. There was more than a little irony in the fact that the very reason my godson wanted to leave The Welcome was the one factor which might have persuaded me to try and suppress the Dennis incident and stay on!

Benjamin got his way. Which meant that I did too. Before lunch we had already booked in at the Négresco—to the evident delight of Jacqueline and Helen, the satisfaction we'd quit the Welcome finally confessed by Benjamin, and the qualified enthusiasm of Ken *after* he had discovered a performance that night of Massenet's *Thaïs* at the Nice opera house.

Derek was not in evidence when we met in the foyer later that afternoon. His mother informed me that she thought he was still in their room unpacking but I had a sneaking suspicion he was already on a bus heading back to the fishing port we'd recently vacated for fond farewells to his girlfriend of twenty-four hours!

I never asked the young man so I do not know for certain. However, his presence was evident late that afternoon when the whole sextet of us (avoiding the *Promenade des Anglais*, jammed with rush-hour traffic) sauntered instead across the palm-lined square of the War Memorial and finally stopped to allow Helen buy Derek a smart leather bag in one of the boutiques on the Place Messina.

Our destination was the further end of the Flower Market where both the opera house and a fish restaurant I knew were situated. We had decided to eat prior to Ken's attendance at *Thaïs* when the boys and their mothers would attend a movie.

But the prior goal on our evening stroll was a suitable café for an apéritif before we patronized *La Flûte Enchantée.* I also wanted to ascertain the time the opera got out so I could meet Ken and walk back to the hotel with him. I had not as yet planned what to do with the few hours suddenly at my disposal.

As the others meandered along the vegetable-strewn lane which bordered the flower market where the stalls were in process of being dismantled, I stopped at the opera foyer for signs of a schedule. Our group was now scattered with the two youngsters taking up the rear and Ken and the mothers some yards ahead. I darted a look backwards as I was about to mount the few steps—just in time to see Derek and Benjamin enter the public convenience on the market side of the narrow thoroughfare.

Not wanting either to lose sight of the adults ahead, or have the boys fail to see me when they left the john, I hovered hesitantly there on the pavement. It seemed ages but could have only been a matter of minutes before my godson and his friend re-emerged. Benjamin was first, followed by a red-faced and obviously discountenanced Derek. From behind there came shouting and at that moment Benjamin raised his fist and yelled something back in angry response.

I had no need to be told what had happened. A huge rage began to expand in me. Benjamin couldn't wait to reach me before he was panting his explanation.

"There was a man in there, Uncle Davey. He kept pushing against Derek—and—and there was something else. Then Derek punched the bastard and we got away."

My temper exploded just as Derek arrived. The igniting fuel may well have contained ingredients as disparate as the expression on Derek's face at *le petit déjeuner* at the Welcome that morning and some resentment that Ken had chosen to attend the opera that night and leave me alone. I am only sure that I experienced a keen sense of protection for the boy as well as disgust at the cameo Ben's words lit in my mind's eye.

Nothing came out as I intended. I had meant to demonstrate a kind of vicarious paternalism—a sense of standing in for the absent Gordon. Instead I raged at his son.

"You idiot," I screamed. "What the hell did you want to go in there for? You could've been knifed, you young fool! Will you get it into your stupid head that this isn't Vancouver? Forget about that damn girl in the *darse* and concentrate on the fact people aren't shocked by what you saw going on in that *pissoir.* This is the Mediterranean, not Presbyterian Scotland, for Chrissakes! That kind of casual hand-sex means nothing to them. They don't hit out at one another because someone's got a hard-on. Or if they do it's with a stiletto in their hand."

Then I could have bitten off my tongue. Derek's eyes began to well. I wasn't sure whether from the experience in the lavatory or from my upbraiding. Then sight of that lanky Anglo-Saxon youth about to erupt in sobbing—with a gathering knot of swarthy *Niçois* throwing him contemptuous glances—or so I interpret it—was more than I could handle. I switched abruptly.

"Come on, old son," I said gently, "We don't want a scene out here, do we? And your mother and the others will be wondering what on earth has happened. I shouldn't say anything to them if I were you. It would only make her worry. You, too, Benjamin. Nothing. okay?"

Jesus! What a hypocrite I could be, I told myself. Did I really care a tinker's fuck whether Helen would worry? In any event, I need not have worried. The boys miraculously pulled themselves together and said nothing to either parent—at least in earshot of me. Whatever hypocrisy I'd been guilty of I was due to pay for before the day ended.

. . .

I still had an hour or so to kill before meeting Ken so was sitting sipping a bright yellow *suze* at a working-class café the far side of the flower market. I had chosen the place with some deliberation. The neighbourhood was one frequented by Algerians and I felt particularly drawn to them and their shy smiles at eye contact which I fancied had as much to do with the arcane mores of the Muslim land over the water as to my overtures.

On a previous visit, when I had shed the company of Cousin Loveday and Tim for an evening alone in Nice, I had responded to one such steadfast smile by following its owner from near where I was now sitting to a vast shanty town on the outskirts where seemingly thousands of dusky immigrants lived in corrugated squalor. I had followed the man to his own shack and, without a word exchanged, spent the night in sexual embrace. The memory was a cherished one and there can be no doubt that erotic promptings, even a half-hearted hope for a repeat experience, moved in me that night. But I rationalized to myself that I had grown sick of the tourist veneer of the city and needed some contact with these exploited remnants of the old French Empire as antidote to the falsity.

Or so the justification went. I was in fact staring hard at a blue-smocked Algerian youth who was returning my meaningful looks from under his tight black curly hair, as I frantically thought how I could turn the exchange to erotic advantage in the short time left before I'd promised Ken we'd meet outside the opera house.

I thought I was about to succumb to a second heart attack when I was addressed in English from the dark of the narrow street.

"Can I join you?"

It was the figure of Derek Goddard, there in the shadows.

"Of course. How the hell did you—"

From the corner of my eye I saw the Algerian youth stand up and move in to the interior of the crowded café. I noted that Derek also watched his progress.

"I followed you. I decided I didn't want to see the movie with the others. In fact I was going back to Villefranche. I'd more or less promised Muriel. But after this afternoon—well, I knew I had to speak to you before anything else."

I was still hot with embarrassment over the Algerian at the next table and couldn't be sure whether Derek had seen me follow him into the café.

"I always like a long, cool drink at a café table when I want to do some thinking. It's one of the things I miss most in Vancouver."

He stared down at my slim glass of half drunk *suze.* I looked at his hand which he'd laid, splayed, on the flaking metal tabletop. I couldn't help noticing how stubby his fingers were. And that he bit his nails.

"I guess you can see what's going on from sitting here and pick up what you like. I bet it's what my Dad would be doing if he were here. At least it's better than that stinking john I was in with Ben. Or that place he goes to at home. The Shannon Steam Baths, 1884 Muir Street. Telephone, 299-6404."

I didn't *want* to believe what I was hearing but there was no escaping the grating misery in his voice. I refused to look up and register a consonant expression on his baby face. It was like driving a speeding auto and discovering it had failed brakes. I wrestled for demeanor but nothing apposite would come. I could barely find breath.

"Did you follow him?" I asked dully.

"Matches. He's always leaving matches around. Steambaths, it said. Right there on the cover. I knew he was a queer before, of course. But not that he went to places like *that.* What—why does it have to be my father? That's what I want to know. And after this afternoon—well—what I wanted to ask you. Well . . . like—"

"Yes, Derek," I coaxed, gentle now with his confusion.

"Could that guy in the john start on me because—because he thinks *I'm* that way? I mean if my Dad . . . Can that stuff be passed on?"

"I've never heard of gayness being hereditary, Derek. So you can put it out of mind."

He wasn't at all satisfied. Not by a long shot.

"My Dad never used to be like that. Not when I was a little kid growing up. He was just a normal father then."

"So what are you suggesting?"

Derek clenched his hand on the table and he spoke with a voice not so much calm as cold. " Maybe you two have made him like it, eh? It's what you and Ken do, isn't it?"

"*Made* him like it," I echoed. "How come?" My voice approached his in needle precision. "What the fuck do you mean by that?"

"You're older than he is, aren't you? And he's always listening to the two of you."

"It isn't measles we're talking about," I told him, "And your father presumably has a will of his own."

"I think Mum suspects. It's breaking her heart. That's why Dad and she have split up. That's why she's here with me. Did you know that?"

"I'll tell you exactly what I know. Your father loves both you and your mother very much indeed. That's why he had a nervous breakdown."

With the abruptness of youth he quit the topic of his father. Switched back to himself. "There was something else about this afternoon. In that toilet."

This time I didn't interrupt.

"The trouble is I *did* look at that guy next to me. I did want to see his thing."

I couldn't let him go on torturing himself. "Curiosity isn't the same as gayness, Derek."

But he brushed that aside, the bit of confession now firmly between his teeth. "For all I know Ben was straining to look as well. After all, his Dad's one, isn't he? But if I am I think I'd kill myself. I wouldn't want to live with that."

Mercifully the waiter returned for fresh orders. Derek refused anything but I asked for a refill of my just drained glass. When the white-coated figure departed I returned reluctantly to replies for this totally bewildered kid.

"Jesus, Derek! Talk about getting things out of proportion! So Ben's father and yours have something in common. You'll have to learn to accept coincidence in this world without making wild constructions out of the fact."

"There's you and Ken," he persisted. "Like it's most of the older men I know. So why shouldn't it be me, then? Mum has a cousin who isn't married—I found that out when we were in England. There's Mr. Beasely, our twelfth grade French teacher, your friends John and Ralph—I don't know their surnames—And I can do perfect take-offs of Carol Burnett and Cleo Laine. Ask Mum and Dad."

"Sitting behind me and over there to the left are four women. Did you notice them when you came to this table? Anything special, that is?"

He shook his head. "Only that they were laughing a lot right? And maybe they were talking some foreign language. Not French or English, I mean. They seemed to be having fun."

"You'll make a detective yet! Now I think, Derek—mind you, I only *think*—that they're lesbians. That they're two pairs. Lovers. Understand?"

He nodded. I wasn't sure that he did, but I still went on. "Now that doesn't turn this café into a gay bar. Nor does it make all Niçoises dykes. And if they're speaking German Swiss, which I think they are—it doesn't make the women of German-speaking Switzerland all lesbians either."

He nodded again, as if digesting something— though unsure what.

"Labels are easy to hand out, but they don't always mean too much. If your father and mother have a problem between them they'll have to work it out in their own way. Name calling won't help. Nor will mentioning everyone they've met through Ken and me. Just because the two of us are gay" (I was acutely aware I'd never talked like this to a friend's son before) "it doesn't mean *all* our male friends—whether they're husbands and fathers or not—are also that way. So please don't jump to a million conclusions, young man!"

I was beginning to feel a little more controlled, more confident in delivering Lesson # 1 in *Gay Understanding*, as Derek sat there staring moodily at the occupants of the adjacent tables.

I followed his gaze. It occurred to me that perhaps the place was a little more gay than I'd supposed. At more than one table were groups of men and at two they consisted of mixed Algerians and Frenchmen.

"I hate it here," my companion said suddenly.

"Let's go somewhere else, then. Perhaps closer to the opera house?"

But I'd completely misunderstood him. "I mean France. Like Lyons and now here in Nice. Everyone's looking at you all the time."

"You should be flattered," I rejoined. "Who knows, maybe Muriel isn't the only young lady to think you're good looking."

He was having no banter. "It isn't like that. It's creepy. They're summing you up all the time. And it's not just the girls, either. It isn't like that back home."

"*Vive la différence*," I persisted blithely—determined to shake him out of his negative mood. "I guess people are a little more *brazen* in their actions in these parts. It could also be called being more honest."

"I still haven't said what I followed you to tell you most of all."

I twirled my *suze* in silence. My experience has always been that when people are determined on confessions—however lengthy the prevarications and false starts—they generally succeed in unloading them.

"I told Ben and he said that I must tell you to your face."

Still I waited. (Though chalking one up for my godson.)

"I hate queerness, Uncle Davey." He clenched his jaw with the difficulty of proceeding. "I suppose what I mean is that even if I am one, I hate queers—like my Dad and—"

"I get the message," I said quietly.

"The point is I want to ask Mum if she and I can leave the rest of you here and I know she won't hear of it unless you help to persuade her. We could fly right to London from here in Nice. I looked it up tonight in the hotel. And from there we can take an earlier Wardair charter."

"All because you hate queers?"

"I don't like France either. And from what you and Uncle Ken said, I think I'd hate Spain even more. These Europeans are all *creeps*. I can tell they hate us by the way they look."

"Let's try and think all this through a bit more," I suggested. "The first thing, Derek, is to be sure you're using the exact words. You know, you have a perfect right to dislike queers, as you call us. No one should call you on that. But hate's something else again. That's a large package of emotions to haul around. Frankly, I don't think you hate your Dad. Nor do I think you hate France. And what with the trouble between your parents, your anxieties over meeting up with Muriel only to have to leave her again so soon—plus being in Europe for the first time—isn't very helpful either. I guess when we're feeling a bit wounded and frustrated, the old familiar paths are what we want most. I'm sure you've already planned to find your way to Kingston when back in Canada, huh?"

By the look I received I knew I'd hit target. That inspired me to continue. I drew breath. "But all that's only part of this particular business, isn't it?"

He looked suspicious. "What do you mean?"

"Well, everything you've just said is from *your* angle. Don't you think your mother has a say, too? And for that matter, the rest of us—including your friend, Ben? By pulling out right now you'll be screwing things up for everyone else. Couldn't you possibly live with the problem for a few days more? That would be the generous thing to do—and I think I know you well enough to know you want to do the really decent thing."

I felt like a scout-master or school chaplain but I had a hunch that young Derek would prefer such old-fashioned talk rather than jargon from a psychiatrist or high school counsellor.

"How much longer are we supposed to stay around here, then?" he asked—and in doing so tacitly complied with my suggestion.

But I was still talking to an impatient and mixed-up eighteen-year-old and I realized it was time for a quick concession from me.

"I personally think we should stay an extra day here—so that you can more or less settle things with Muriel rather than rushing off and leaving a slew of loose strings. Then we might call a party conference and decide what we *all* want to do next. If we went further along the coast you might just persuade Muriel's parents to let her join us. There's lots of things we might work out."

I was bloody certain there was no way that mad Dennis would let his daughter out of his sight to accompany us. But I was not about to air my convictions as it was obvious the boy needed all the hope he could muster. In the event, he said goodbye to Muriel—with the two of them rashly promising to subsequently meet each other when back in Canada, as I'd surmised.

Two days later, after some tedious flopping on the beach and being duly baked by the sun, we drove on to Cannes and Marseilles. It was there the boys persuaded their mothers to let them take a small ship to Barcelona where we would await them. We were thus reduced to a comfortable four in our slow progression across southern France in the rented car.

FIFTEEN

≈

Barcelona proved the zenith of our European vacation which concluded in as genuine high affection and enthusiasm as it had started in Paris. The sea voyage certainly proved beneficial to Derek who not only made no immediate reference to our *tête-à-tête* in Nice but seemed to go out of his way to be considerate to Ken and me. I was distinctly flattered and Ken several times repeated himself in observing what a pleasant young man Derek had become over the past year or so.

But I cannot ascribe the euphoric mood which enveloped me in the Mediterranean's largest city as exclusively the fruits of our reunion as a group or the behavior of any constituent of it. The fact was I enjoyed Barcelona which trod closely on the heels of Lyons as being my favourite European city. I have always felt buoyant in its environs.

It is not necessary to probe deep into the realms of self-knowledge to ascertain why. I had visited the place since my late teens and even earlier had read of its Civil War history with admiration bordering on awe. It was where I had taken student vacations from both London and Lyons and in spite of the *Falangist* puritanism which had maintained gender-divided beaches and dealt savagely with gay activity, I had made close friends with a handsome member of the *Guardia Civil* who subsequently took a wife and fathered three children.

It was through Alfredo that I met Alberto—and had one of those febrile adolescent love affairs (throughout the August of 1947) which now made me so sympathetic to the lovelorn Derek having to abandon his Muriel for what must have seemed like eternity.

But Barcelona was more than a memory of happy lust and ardent love. Alberto had been a poet: a Catalan nationalist who delighted in teaching me the linguistic equivalent of the hated Spanish and fired me with anecdotes of heroism by his extended anti-Fascist family during the Civil War.

In my adolescence I was ever seeking to identify with those whom I admired and it wasn't difficult for a romantic Cornishman, only too aware of the heavy hand of the English, to do so there in the capital of

Catalonia. I was sorry when I learned that Catalan was another Romance language and not a Celtic one, yet it didn't mitigate my devotion to these imprudent sons of a small, economically unviable country which the stern rules of history dictated was doomed to culturally disappear as our Cornish Principality already had.

Nor did my pleasure and admiration of Barcelona conclude on that note of parallel nationalism. Like Lyons, it was not a superficially attractive city. Like Lyons, it had a business-life of its own; carried on with a splendid indifference to those who might be visiting it. In other words (unlike Cornwall) it was immune to the blandishments of the tourist industry. I would have surrendered to that fact alone!

Barcelona—industrially busy, Catalan hectic and Catalan sad; old enough to ache and young enough to chafe—I responded once more to its dubious mix and delighted in showing and sharing such places as the Ramblas, with its cruel echoes of Bedlam, the brash insolence of Gaudi's architecture and the stolid medievalism of the Benedictine abbey of Montserrat beyond the city's hem.

On our very first day we sat at a café table where years earlier I'd left a purse—only to find it where I'd left it an hour or so later, untouched and unemptied. Ken and I tried to explain how although the end of Franco's regime was ardently welcome, and the new dishonesty (that purse of mine would've been stolen now within *seconds*) lamentable, the two things didn't cancel each other out.

It wasn't easy to explain to our two pragmatic and unhistorical young men. In many respects it was this kind of thing which made me feel isolated from both of them—much more than the distinctions of age and sexual divergence.

Maybe I was still smarting over Derek's words to me in the café and Benjamin's prissy reaction to the well-hung waiter at the Welcome. In any case, it was soon apparent they were bored with my elaborate homily over the moral dilemmas of politics. After exchanging glances they politely asked permission to leave.

The four of us watched them saunter off down the Ramblas in the direction of the beach at San Sebastián where I suspected they wanted to swim.

"I've bored the tits off them," I commented wryly. "God! That's an apolitical generation coming up!"

"You're too earnest," Jacqueline said. "Benjamin just hates anything so head-on. I suppose he's learned to duck outright arguments. He's got his father to thank for that—you know it isn't me! It's only by dodging unpleasant truths about things that he's learned to live with himself."

"You musn't take it so personally, Davey," Helen said. "They're still kids. I mean, seventeen and eighteen. You should have more faith in them. They'll come around in their own way."

"That's just what worries me. Already in their late teens and they still don't seem to have a clue! Youngsters their age were fighting here in the streets of Barcelona for what they believed in—just a few years ago!"

"Would you want Ben and Derek doing that? Is that what you really want?" Jacqueline asked, a rasp of irritation in her throat.

Now it was time to get mad with the mothers. I detested the kind of solidarity they exhibited because one deigned to criticize their offspring! It denied the friendship I had with them as women and allowed them to cast me as just a well-meaning outsider.

As usual, I took the path of the personal and particular in my attack. "Right in the direction they're now walking, below the promenade, there used to be a line of bathing huts—where *El Caudillo* allowed the Spanish male to undress and put on a swimsuit that covered the whole body before wading onto his separated section of the beach."

"I would have thought *you'd* have gone for that," Helen wickedly interjected. I was in no mood for smart-ass comments from her.

"I was slightly younger than your son when I entered one of those cabins and saw scrawled on the wall: *Viva El Homosexualismo!* I'd already seen the *Guardia Civil* at work arresting gays. I knew precisely just how much daring went into that graffiti—and the price that would have to be paid. Or do you want me to tell you about the bunch I saw roughing up a gay kid outside a sentry box by the barracks? They were soldiers and they were using their rifle butts. They were actually enjoying drawing blood in full daylight—to the approval of a bunch of civilians and a *Guardia Civil* in his stupid three-cornered hat, who stood there grinning. Then this was the Spain of Francisco Fucking Franco! That kind of thing was encouraged, not just tolerated!"

"Davey has a point," Ken said. "Christ! These kids have to be told something of what's happened before they were born. It's their century, too, you know! I'm sorry if we sound a bit of a bore on the subject but I think you'd find blacks tend to go on about being blacks in a white world and Jews *know* they must never forget how Gentiles bite when least expected."

"We're discussing two boys whose fathers could be imprisoned, fired from their jobs at any time," I said. "Don't you think they should be made aware of those dangers?"

The atmosphere was suddenly very tense. I knew precisely how many taboo topics I'd kicked into life.

"Well, I don't propose to discuss Neil's indecent exposure and cavorting with a minor. Certainly not here in a Barcelona café where I'm supposed to be on vacation. I know you love these heavy sessions, Davey. But I can do without yet another sermon on persecuted gays every time we sit down and the conversation flags! I guess I should be grateful you didn't bring it up when we were driving all that distance in the car."

"If I'd known you were so bothered by the subject, I'd have made sure we were not in a position for it to have happened. It's enough to have bigots like Doug Collins back home—or homophobes like that creep from Kingston we left behind in Villefranche. I'm buggered if I'm going to put up with it here." I sprang to my feet.

It was Helen who put out a restraining hand. "Let's all keep our cool, shall we? If we were anti-gay, Davey, would we be here with you—even dragging along our good-looking if politically stupid sons?"

Dearest Helen! How could I resist her words? I sighed and sat down again. "You're right, Mrs. Goddard. I was being stupid. Kiss and make up?"

"And so were *we* idiots," conceded Helen, "for being bloody defensive about the boys. You know, there are times I feel like slitting my throat when I hear myself going on like a stage mother."

Jacqueline took my left hand, and Ken's in her other one. "Let me say something, may I? I think Helen will agree. In fact I *know* she will because we've discussed it before."

We sat waiting. A trifle self-conscious, I suppose. But not too much. At times like this Jacqueline came across as very French and we all, Anglo-Saxonly, gave her a leeway which I suspect we would have denied ourselves.

"I don't have to tell you there's a hell of a lot for Neil and me still to work out—that is if we can. And I never for a moment forget that he's Benjamin's dad. It's the same with Helen. I think we women have really good relationships with our sons. And Helen and Gordon have a more open thing going than I do with you-know-whom. But when all that's said and done we have a special relationship with the two of you. Sitting around this table, we make a foursome—whether anyone outside understands it or not."

I don't think I ever felt closer to Jacqueline than then. Or with Helen, for that matter.

How to put it without sounding corny? However much Ken and I defended their husbands through the ties of gay bonding, Jacqueline and Helen were our friends for their own sakes. I didn't forget the particular links between Neil and my lover—that was rather like that between Helen and Jacqueline. And poor Gordon's self-hatred and split between his love of his son and the need to be fucked, could make me feel so protective I wanted to cry.

But beyond the plight of the men and the fragile place thus allotted their sons, these women stood apart: people skilled in picking up human pieces, of absorbing pain and with an ability mounting to genius for placing their feet in the imprint of others.

How much this was the general skill of women, and how much the unique traits of my two mother-buddies, I was incapable of telling. I strove for words that wouldn't sound too sentimental. My mind was all turmoil: the matter too heavy.

It was Ken, wittingly or otherwise, who came to my rescue. "I think it's time we planned an expedition to Montserrat to see the famous Black Madonna."

"The Black Madonna," we murmured back—rather fatuously, as if replying to some weird kind of toast.

That was the last specific site we visited and I think the boys enjoyed the hike up to it, even if there were several British Columbian sneers over what Catalonians were content to describe as a mountain. The monastery scarcely impinged on them while they didn't bother at all with the church and the black effigy of the Blessed Virgin.

Where the two unequivocally enjoyed themselves was when we left the city for the Costa Brava and the fishing village-cum-resorts of Blanes and Tossa del Mar, huddled so picturesquely by the vaunted blue sea.

Again I felt it was some specious magazine allure which captivated them but by that stage in our collective sojourn I think we had all acquired a measure of mutual tolerance. Not only did I refrain from comment but I actively shared in their games and did my best to identify with their fun.

I am understating. For once in my life I actually enjoyed lying there in the hot silver sand, as the two of them pranced about with a huge coloured ball rented from the beach concession for a few pesetas. From somewhere—I suspect on the boat that had conveyed them from Marseilles—they had both procured swimsuits of such scanty proportions their manufacture could only be French. They were, in fact, little more than genital pouches with the scarlet material of Benjamin's and the bright green of Derek's, disappearing at the back up the crack of their buttocks.

By this stage in the holiday both lads were deeply suntanned—with my brunet godson transformed into a dark-honeyed adonis and his slightly older friend of almost equal splendour. I stirred restlessly. This was the second time there on the Costa Brava that my thoughts about the sons of my friends had abruptly taken a lewd turn. The previous afternoon, when fooling in the startlingly blue water with Ben who had begged me to constantly surface dive between his legs, I had found the sensation of sliding between his thighs far too attractive. However, that at least had been in the safety of the sea. There was no protection lying there on the beach and when I looked down at my own, albeit more conservative swim trunks, I had embarrassing occasion to turn over on my tummy and hide my arousal from the dangers of passing Mums.

It was the very first time in sixteen years that I had responded to Benjamin in this manner and I was both shocked and disturbed. As soon as I felt my tumescent cock relax into something more like a flaccid penis I scampered to my feet and beat a retreat to the multi-coloured umbrella where I had left Ken and the women sprawled out.

I prudently stayed with my peers until eventually, after a deliciously late meal of mochas and scampi, we were finally able to say goodnight and escape to our hotel room. At first I wasn't going to tell my bedmate but that resolution proved as vain as the vast majority of others in similar idiom I had made over the years to Ken. We were hardly between the sheets before it all gushed out.

"I nearly made a fool of myself over Benjamin this afternoon. If I didn't know it was an old wives' tale I'd say I'd been bitten by Spanish fly—even though this is Catalonia!"

"Funnee! You don't mean to tell me you were tempted to tell him you were gay or anything like that?"

"Be serious. This wasn't funny. Though, really, I had no choice in the matter. It wasn't as if I *plotted* anything. It was just watching the two of them play with that fucking beach ball."

"So you had a conditioned reflex? You suddenly found yourself in a state of sexual stimulus by watching golden youth at play?"

That silenced me. "How do you know?"

"Well, you're not quite senile yet. Nor do you own a seeing eye dog. In fact you're what might be called a perfectly normal faggot. Why wouldn't you respond with a hard-on to observing two handsome young men in a state of semi-nudity throwing their baskets in your direction as you lie in the warm sand fantasizing? If you were to tell me you remained as limp as a dishrag between your legs when they came on in those wicked little briefs, then I really would start worrying!"

"I came up the beach as soon as I realized what was happening. I tell you, I was terrified that dear Jacqueline with her ferret eyes would drop by."

"You needn't have come up the beach. That was my mistake."

"I don't get you."

"I went up as soon as I discerned tremors between my thighs. I didn't realize that it was only to exchange the temptations of the eye in terms of their offspring for a lascivious comparison of the equipment of the Catalan fishermen in the café last night, with these gorgeous types spreading their legs all over the bloody beach! My God! Those women are *experts!* I might just as well have stayed closer to the water and mentally enjoyed their sons as I presumed you were doing. Only I thought you'd have enough sense to lie on your tummy *below* where they were playing. That way you could have quietly screwed the beach as you watched them. Of course, you'd have had to plunge back into the Med afterwards to cover up your *tache d'amour* with a general wetness, you know."

"No, I didn't know. Nor did I know what an old reprobate existed under the guise of that innocent face with the air of a gentle professor. I don't think I have ever heard you speak so lewdly before, Kenneth. Really I haven't!"

But Ken wasn't going to rise to my banter. Instead, he carried on as if I'd begged him for an erotic re-enactment of the beach events that afternoon.

"Now while you were grinding your iron-hard tool into the beach of Tossa del Mar, what do you think was going on in those two boys' heads?"

"If you think for one moment they knew I had a hard-on you're mistaken. I was over on my stomach in a flash. Besides, they could've cared less. There's lovelorn Derek languishing for Muriel back in Villefranche and Benjamin whom I doubt is much past jacking off to photos from *Playboy*."

"Bullshit! But leave Ben out of it for the moment. I'm not saying it was deliberate but consciously or otherwise, those two lads were *flirting*—first with me and then with you. It had to be. There was no one else near them on the beach. And that, my dear, certainly includes girls. If you didn't deliberately get an erection then you must also realize that young males don't deliberately flirt either. They can't help it. They know they're cute, they know they're well-endowed, and they know we invariably respond. They're prisoners of flattery, that's all!"

"It's still alarming. I mean, randy thoughts about boys who are almost your own kids! Isn't there such a thing as *spiritual* incest? We're getting into ugly things here."

"I'm still not through with *deliberate* and what that means," Ken said—in a voice I recognized as meaning however much I interrupted him, he'd come back to the same point! I shut up.

"None of us is responsible for what swims into our minds," he went on. "But we are for how we act on it."

"You sound like all those silly Catholics, Anglican and Roman, who want us to be more celibate than the priesthood—especially more celibate than the married Anglicans and the *Uniate* Papists," I added. "I thought there was something in the Bible about *If thine eye offend thee, pluck it out*?"

"I wouldn't know. You're the theologian. Anyway, this goes beyond anything gay. You can be awfully naïve, Davey. Didn't you know that lots of straight fathers have fleeting erotic thoughts about their daughters? But they don't all commit incest. And that goes for Uncles over nubile nieces, sisters over brothers. Nor is it only sexual. People have the most awful thoughts of violence over loved ones they'd die defending from harm. And obscene images too. I mean, every kid has had thoughts about his parents screwing or dumping or what have you—and felt flustered by it. There's no end to the flotsam that swims into our minds. It's just the sieve which ensures it isn't acted on that counts."

I could be as obstinate as my lover. "I still don't like seeing my godson as a sex object. It's never happened before and I'd like to make sure it doesn't again."

"Then I suggest you keep off the beach and make sure his mother's always around. And knowing Benjamin you'd better tell him to steer clear of his randy Uncle Davey—which will be hard for him at his age as he loves to flirt, as I told you."

The conversation between us became progressively desultory, partly because I'd run out of steam and partly because we were both now ready to tightly embrace. I was also aware that if I pushed my side of the argument too hard I was in danger of looking ridiculous. And even after years of living with Ken I hated losing an argument to him.

Mercifully the next morning took us away from the temptations of beach life and with the car duly packed and the six of us ensconced, we headed north for Paris and a quite different set of complications.

SIXTEEN

≈

We had just passed through the river town of Agen and were heading north of the Garonne in the direction of Périgord where Ken had promised to host lunch when I grew aware of trouble in the back seat. That was not totally surprising. The boys often sparred with one another while their mothers (especially in the mornings) were of uncertain temper and inclined to lash out at their offspring, regardless of who was at fault.

On this, the penultimate morning of our time together, the explosion took a different turn and involved the two Goddards rather than the more mercurial Jacqueline and Benjamin. The latter were amiably arguing, as I recall, from front seat to back, whose turn it next was to sit by Ken (I was driving) when Helen's voice abruptly crescendoed.

"No you bloody well can't go back to Villefranche and for Christ's sake stop bugging me. You've been whining since Barcelona. I'm sick to death of it!"

She fell silent again—as if afraid to say too much. Which was not a usual fear with her! I glanced at the driving mirror. Derek was sitting hunched and unhappy in the corner. It wasn't hard to guess the motivation behind the desire to return to Villefranche.

His mother, of course, saw it exclusively in terms of young Muriel and therefore nursed a maternal protectiveness over her boy. No matter that other mothers stood in eternal guard over their daughters—the Helens of this world are convinced it is Eve-the-Siren, regardless of age, who remains the snare and temptress of their guileless sons.

Then Helen had not been privy to my conversation with Derek in Nice. I was certain that, to a purely physical attraction for the Woolnough girl, had been added a yearning to prove his heterosexuality. It had been the case with plenty of older men I'd known—and given a boy with the knowledge Derek had of his father—he could hardly be blamed for his mixture of motives.

It was impossible for me to intervene as I'd promised him our conversation would be totally confidential. To complicate things, his mother found second breath and decided to involve all of us.

"Do you know what my son has done? He's written a stupid note to his father saying he's met the love of his life and that I'm doing my best to destroy it. I ask you!"

"Mum! That's not fair!"

"Who's asking what's fair? That sex-starved little puss isn't fair. Come to that, I don't think a letter to someone who's himself a sexual mess and is in the middle of a nervous breakdown was fair either!"

"I only want to go down there for a day or so before we go back. The Woolnoughs asked me so it wouldn't cost anything. I'd hitchhike."

"That's not the point."

"No, I know what the point is. You're jealous. That's what's really the matter!"

"Me jealous? Of you?" Helen made no attempt to conceal the scorn.

I knew her son well enough to intercept the slight tremor in his response. He knew he was risking things.

"Of Muriel and me. Of what we feel for each other. You and Dad are—"

"Over the hump?" she put in quickly. Too quickly. "Don't be ridiculous!"

"I didn't say that," he retorted. "I mean if Dad doesn't . . . Well, if you and he don't. I'm not an idiot you know."

It was then she broke. "Stop it! I won't listen to you! You know nothing whatever about it. How dare you mention things that are nothing to do with you!"

"You stupid cow! It's got everything to do with me!"

I let my foot off the accelerator. "Shut up both of you or I'll stop the car. I don't want to hear any more."

Jacqueline came to my rescue. "Stop it, Derek. This isn't the time."

"Or the place, old chap," Ken added, turning and smiling at the boy. "Those are hard things. They can't be turned into car chit-chat."

I tried to backtrack. "Or even automotive ammunition!"

"I didn't start it," the boy said sullenly.

But that was it. He said no more. Not even when the atmosphere slackened a little and there were various attempts to change the subject. Nor did he speak much during lunch in Périgeux when we were all phonily jocose and laughed excessively.

The afternoon, though, seemed better. Derek actually told a story about the two of them on the boat from Marseilles to Barcelona—something involving him ordering *ris de veau* which they both thought was a rice dish and being distressed to hear from a Brit at their table that it was sweetbreads in English and further horrified to learn it was the pancreas in medicine.

By this time on our trip various little liturgies had been forged. One of them was an assembly at seven o'clock for drinks before dinner. In the small village of Randanne on the outskirts of Clermont-Ferrand, where we'd decided to stop for the night, I quickly registered that the women came down to the tiny bar of the Coq d'Or wearing dresses and had spruced themselves up more than usual. This was to be our last evening together as Jacqueline and Benjamin were going to be left off in Lyons the next day.

We didn't sit in the bar but on the cramped sidewalk outside. This was the threshold to an ancient bridge which slowed the stream of traffic and provided us with both an excess of noise and the stench of diesel fumes from the giant trucks heading for industrial Clermont Ferrand, or on to Lyons.

The Coq d'Or had been chosen by us as it was conveniently opposite the one restaurant in town. However, the line of traffic blocked the place from view and when Ken recalled it had a small garden on the river bank, we decided we'd quit the noise and din and seek shelter across the road where we would at least be able to hear each other speak.

By this time Ken, in a pale blue *tricot* he'd bought in Nice and not worn before, had joined the ladies and me so we all four dodged through the traffic to the orange awning of the incalculably named *Restaurant du Mont Blanc.*

Jacqueline had been on the phone to her mother and reported with mock consternation that every question from the old lady was to do with her grandson and that she wasn't even asked if she was enjoying her vacation. It was obvious that Benjamin had scored a signal success with his grandparents and it was my comparing the situation with the less happy one which had confronted Helen and Derek in Frome, which made me wonder where the two Canadian grandsons were. Neither boy could be called punctual but we had all commented that when food and drink were in the offing they were rarely far away.

The arrival of a waiter bringing menus prompted my asking their whereabouts. Even this was something of a routine as they often took a walk on their own and turned up a trifle late for drinks which patently had less interest for them than us. Ken pointed out that we had agreed to meet at the bar when last together and volunteered to cross back and tell them we'd already gone to the restaurant.

When he returned some ten minutes later he was still alone. He had hardly drawn up to the table when Helen was on her feet and hastening back in the same direction. Eight o'clock came and went before she reappeared. In her hand was a hand-scrawled note on a piece of graph paper torn from the kind of *cahier* French students use for taking notes. Wordlessly she dropped it on the table in front of us.

It was from Derek.

Dear Mum:

I know what I have to do so please don't interfere. This is as good a place as any for me to hitch a ride. I took some money from our pile—also my air ticket home. Say hi to everyone. I'm sorry to have to pull out like this. But in any case it was the end of our trip all together.

See you either at Gatwick or back in Vancouver.

Your loving son, Derek

Scanning the lines, Ken said: "He can't have gotten far."

I jumped up. "If we hurry and drive to the edge of town I'm sure we can find him waiting for a lift out there on the highway."

"You drive out there and we'll check around here," Ken suggested. "By the way, where's Benjamin?"

"Oh God!" his mother exclaimed. "You don't think he's gone, too?"

Helen shook her head. "I'm sure he's helped. They're good friends, after all. But my little boy wants to do this thing on his great big own. Jesus! I hope he doesn't do anything really dumb."

She was obviously trying to keep her voice even, to stay calm. I knew my Helen, though. She kept brushing imaginary hair away from her forehead. Either that, or scratching lightly at the tip of her nose. I remembered our driving out to supper at Peppe's in West Vancouver when she'd divulged her anxieties over Gordon. It was as if no time had elapsed between then and now.

Ken suggested she accompany him to the *Place des Victoires* which was in fact the town square, but she'd have none of it.

"Take Jacqueline. I'll go with Davey."

There were just the first intimations of dusk as she and I drove east towards the highway leading to Clermont-Ferrand, St. Etienne, and Lyons.

"I don't even know how I can stop him. We can't arrest him, you know."

I didn't reply. Just kept searching each side of the deserted street. After a couple of fruitless sorties up and down the road, I pulled into the curb.

"That's up to you, Helen. You'll just have to play it by feel. If I see him I'll just talk until you can join us. Why don't you take this side on foot and I'll cross the street and walk along there?"

With that I leaned over and opened the door for her. I was keen to escape. Not because of the weight of her anxiety but because of my own impotence. Her tension invaded me. I felt so close I wanted to clutch her and banish such things as her guilt and fears. Yet I knew there was no real surrogate role for me. It was only as friend and a baffled one at that, I could serve her. I would try and find her son. I couldn't mend whatever was damaged between them.

I hadn't gone half a block when I was overcome with certainty I would come across Derek. So there was absolutely no shock when I took a few steps up the next dark alley and recognized his white windbreaker in a deserted doorway. Nor did he seem the slightest bit surprised at seeing me.

"Hello. Did she send you after me? I saw the car across the road—was she in there too?"

I nodded. "At this moment she's searching the other side of the street." I could just make out the stubborn jut of his chin. "She's also eating her heart out."

"I don't want to see her. I'm not going to Paris with her—like I said in the letter."

"That's for the two of you to discuss. All I promised is that I'd tell her where you are if I found you."

"Well you haven't found me. And I don't want her to know I'm here. I won't be, anyway, as soon as I pick up a truck."

"It's not quite as easy as that, is it? I mean from my point of view."

"I'm asking you to say you haven't found me. It's nothing really to do with her. But I can't explain that to anyone. Only you understand, Davey. Because of what we talked about there in Nice?"

I nodded. "I thought as much. In fact it's not much to do with Muriel either, is it?"

But he wasn't about to spell things out that succinctly.

"Of course it's to do with Muriel. We've been on the phone several times since I left. It's been hell for her. Her old man has threatened to shoot Henri, the guy with the boat berthed next to theirs. The asshole thinks Henri's trying to seduce Muriel—when in fact he's really interested in Thelma!

"But that's only part of it. Henri's wife, Huguette, is leaving him and Muriel thinks her mother is about to split from Dennis—not just because of Henri but she's tired of being beaten up and fed up with his drunken fits and—"

"And you're going down there like the Lone Ranger to clear up the whole fucking mess? Derek, sweetheart, they'll chew you into hamburger! I've seen that kind of domestic couple before. They're like whirlpools—they can suck the unwary into their vortex in a flash."

"But you haven't felt like I do for Muriel, have you? That's the point. That's the real point."

"I know that people—friends, whatever you like—only try and interfere between warring couples at their peril. I'm not counselling selfishness, Derek. I'm talking survival!"

The truth was we occupied different territories. He wasn't interested in my advice over pastoral strategy. He was talking self-discovery—with Muriel the primary source of revelation.

"It's not just that she needs me. I need her."

I tried another and final tack, even though I didn't feel exactly clean about it.

"Your mother's my friend, you know. I have made her a promise. Do you think I should renege on that?"

He scraped his shoe uneasily on the doorstep. "I don't know anything about that. That's something between you two, I guess. But you're my friend, too. My oldest friend. And I've got to ask you not to tell her I'm here. Not until I'm gone, anyways. Davey, you know about all the other things—about my Dad and that. If you and Ken can't understand and don't help me—who the fuck else do I have?"

I saw that clearly enough; accepted the boy's logic as unassailable. Indeed, I took it one stage further. A rationalization, maybe, but tied deeply to what existed between Helen and me. Derek was her extension, at least in this filial context. I had to help her, this once at least, *through* her son. The truth about himself, his sexual identity, was crucial to his well-being.

All my experience had taught me the bitter cost for those who postponed confrontation of their sexual orientation. Or who willfully repressed the same in youth—to have it surface savagely in middle-age when time had extolled its physical cost and sex had become only a crude purchase or even just a masturbatory longing. Such prices life extolled were not only ugly to behold, but made their victims even uglier than needs be.

I swallowed physically. And in doing so, swallowed my recent promise to Helen.

"All right," I muttered. "I won't tell her I found you. You'd better wait twenty minutes or so before I drive her back to the others."

I meant what I said. But my heart still felt heavy. Nor was its weight assuaged when he impulsively threw his arms about me and kissed me fully on the lips. The stench of Judas, valid or not, hung too thickly on the air for me to savor the caress of his boyish gratitude.

SEVENTEEN

≈

It was not easy keeping my promise to Derek and breaking that to his mother. I am by nature a blabber-mouth and I doubt if I could have sustained my silence without the active support of Ken. As it was, I managed to keep the fact of my meeting the boy even from him until we had left Helen with the two Murphys in Lyons—from where she was going to take the first train possible to Nice—and we were left to ourselves once more as we headed for Paris.

In the car I merely relayed the raw facts to which he replied by saying he didn't really know what else I could've done in the circumstances. It wasn't until we were high over the Arctic headed for home that the subject was truly ventilated—then I always have a better perspective, and can verbally clothe unruly concepts, when I'm over thirty thousand feet and looking down on clouds.

Not only did Ken agree with preserving silence over the meeting with Derek but he insisted I say nothing when we get home—until, that was, Helen had heard from her son.

As things turned out, apart from learning that he had arrived safely in Vancouver from Villefranche (after missing his scheduled connection at Gatwick and thus forfeiting his cheap charter fare), a lengthy discussion of Helen's apparent wild goose chase and Derek's defection was postponed. Other events intervened.

Chief among these involved Neil Murphy. We had only been back a matter of hours when he was on the phone, pleading to come round and see us at once.

Long gone was the legacy of worry over the campus incident. His eyes again sparkled. The gloss had returned to his black curly hair, and he bounced up and down on our chintz sofa as if he were an excited teenager. Indeed, it occurred to me that he now seemed extraordinarily like the young man who had accompanied us through southern France and northern Spain.

So like his son, in fact, that Ken, usually the more discreet, mentioned it at once.

"God, you do look like Benjamin! It's uncanny!"

Neil beamed. "Surely you mean Ben looks like me."

"Whichever," I added, handing him a spritzer, "But it's you who has changed since we left. What is it—a full professorship at UBC or just a facelift?"

He was wearing a yellow lambswool sweater I had not seen before. And green cords, which nicely matched. I had never thought of Neil as a dresser and felt sure this sartorial change had something to do with it.

He wasn't about to hold us in suspense. In fact he couldn't restrain himself another second.

"I've met someone," he said on an out-rush of breath. "I know it sounds perfectly crazy—perhaps even grotesque for a man who won't see forty again—but I'm madly in love."

It flashed through my mind that Neil wouldn't be seeing forty-*four* again either. But he forestalled any bitchy comment.

"What's more it's mutual. Daniel is muggins enough to think I'm right for him, too."

He really did look radiant. In spite of myself, I couldn't help responding to the joy of him.

"It sounds wonderful, Neil. Where did you meet? How old is he? Is he from Vancouver?"

"Whoah! One at a time, please."

Ken's mind seemed to be running on a different track. "Does Jacqueline know the good news?"

I intercepted a look between them. There was no antagonism, nothing remotely judgmental on Ken's part. I think I'd missed the small note of protectiveness in his question—seen only a moral prodding. Not for the first time was I given to underestimate the friendship between these two.

Neil held up his hand and ticked off his fingers. "He's twenty-eight. We met in the shirt department in the Bay." (I was later to be told by Daniel it had been in the third-floor men's washroom.) "And he was born way up north in Burns Lake."

I thought of that harsh little town in the mineral-rich folds of the Skeena Valley; remembered a place of broken glass violence with drunken Indian pitted against drunken white. It was hard to conceive of a place less likely to spawn gays. My interest in the unknown Daniel quickened.

"And his mother is Irish, a Callaghan, which is my grandmother's name, so we think we're related," Neil continued.

Ken raised his eyebrows in mock horror. "My God, incest, too! Where will it ever end?"

"It won't!" said Neil triumphantly. "It's for ever and ever."

I didn't want to quench his ardor, but I couldn't entirely abandon Jacqueline. I remembered our talks about whether she would return to him after the time in Europe.

"There was another question," I blurted. "Ken's."

There was no slackening of buoyancy. "Oh, Jackie? Of course I told her right away. I would've done anyway—but Daniel insisted. He has to have *everything* up front," he added proudly.

"She didn't mind?" I asked. "Took it all in her stride?"

Perhaps there was a faint pause of exasperation then. "Well, she didn't exactly gurgle with joy when I told her. Then nor was Daniel all that happy to hear of her existence."

"It must've come as a shock," Ken said slowly, twirling the ice in his glass. "Especially as she's been debating for weeks whether to return to the house or not."

"Well, all that became academic," Neil said. "But deep down I don't think it was as much of a surprise as you might think. Our marriage had really run out of steam, you know. And although we didn't talk about it very much, we both felt Ben was now old enough to understand things if we should break up."

Over my godson I felt bolder, more honestly angry with Neil. "That was hardly the way he acted when you were caught on campus. I've never seen anyone more miserable. And when we were away he couldn't wait to get back and see you. I'm not kidding, Neil. He told me that to my face. The kid worships you."

"Which perhaps explains why he's decided to stay with Daniel and me. Jacqueline's rented an apartment in Killarney. You know that white building, with pillars like *Tara*, along Point Grey Road? Isn't it a lark, her moving into a place named Killarney? Then I always thought she was more in love with the Irish connection than with me!"

I couldn't pretend his flippancy made me less cross. "How very convenient it's all turned out. A real fairy story with a happy ending! Those things don't happen very often. Not with love-triangles—let alone cross-gender ones."

He wasn't to be rankled—at least by me. "Of course, it's going to cost the earth. I've promised Jacqueline I'll pay the apartment rent and, naturally, for Ben at the University. But all that's only fair. I shall have to provide her with a hefty down-payment too. So Daniel and I will be living off mere pennies at first."

"Talking of Daniel, what does he do?" Ken asked. "I gather he isn't a millionaire."

"He's a restorer," Neil informed us.

I couldn't resist. "Really? Patently not of marriages!"

Neil was no longer smiling as he addressed me. "Of period furniture, old documents, that kind of thing. And if through some profound sense of Cornish loyalty you feel you can only side with Jacqueline by being bitchy to Daniel and me, then that's your privilege, Davey. In which case I shall now go and you can take as read all those cliché things about 'how nice it was knowing you.'"

But it was Ken who got to his feet—not our guest. "Hold your horses, sweetheart. Davey here is just being excessively Cornish. You know how it is. When they face anything the slightest bit unusual they stress all the objections before looking for solutions. There's absolutely no reason why we should turn you and Jacqueline into an either/or situation. In fact I know bloody well we shan't!"

Neil's sudden change in pose had made me rather nervous. It was a side of him with which I wasn't overly familiar. I much preferred the blithe Irish mood to that fleeting glimpse of dark anger.

"I'm sorry, Neil. Ken's right. I'm taking positions when none are needed and regarding Jacqueline as if she weren't her own woman. What I should be saying is when are we going to meet your Daniel?"

Neil was immediately mollified. Then I have never known him stay ruffled for very long or dream of harbouring a grudge. He was and is one of the most ebullient people I know.

"Jacqueline and I are still real friends. We are also the father and mother of a darling son. Nothing can alter that or break the bonds of parenthood and nearly twenty years living together. I can only *tell* you that now. You'll just have to wait to see it work out in practise."

I hung my head. I believed him.

"Now when do you want to see Daniel?"

My contrition begat enthusiasm. "Now! Right away! Where is he?"

My lover, ever the more equitable, the less compulsive, smiled broadly. "Whenever is convenient for the two of you, of course. We haven't settled into our routine yet. Don't go dragging him away from something he's busy with just for us, though. I know you!"

"He's at home waiting. I wanted him to come with me but he refused. He went on like you are, about making sure it was convenient."

I'm sure it is the demand for immediacy which I share with Neil that accounts for much of Ken's affection towards both of us. It was certainly a case of opposite traits attracting as he rarely exhibited the kind of impulsiveness which has so often landed Neil and me in trouble.

"Why not call him, then?" Ken said. "You're obviously going to be impossible until we've met him."

Neil crossed the carpet and kissed him before picking up the phone. When he sat down again he stretched out his arms as if metaphorically inviting us to him.

"The incredible thing, the utterly marvelous thing, is that Benjamin and Daniel took to one another right away. At first I thought it was just to please me—then I thought it might be just to annoy his mother."

"You always were capable of most unworthy suspicions," Ken chided.

I agreed. "People can be so much bigger than we think. Jacqueline especially. Particularly when she isn't feeling threatened."

"Bull's eye!" Neil exclaimed. "I could hardly believe my luck. But I don't think for a moment Jackie sees Daniel as any kind of competition. It's somehow all on a different plane. She's always seen my gayness as something on the side—peripheral to her, that is."

"Well, if we're going to use big words, let me be cynical and say most people can afford to be magnanimous—when it doesn't impinge too hard on themselves." Ken wagged a finger at our guest. "You are always marvelously tolerant of your colleagues in the Department when they're being unfaithful to their partners!"

I couldn't let that pass. "Now it's you being unfair, Ken! I've heard your pal, here, foam at the mouth about old goat profs screwing everything in sight—including students when they got the chance."

Neil ignored all that. "As I said earlier, I don't want to give the impression Jacqueline is humming with happiness over what happened. I know it was a shock for her."

"She can hardly be blamed!" Ken commented.

Before the topic of Jacqueline could again be recycled, the doorbell rang. Neil jumped to his feet and crossed the room to answer it.

Over his shoulder he shouted to us on the sofa. "Don't worry. I'll get it. He must've been just waiting for me to call, and then come speeding down Ninth Avenue!"

I scarcely had time to get up before he was back, his arm tight around the shoulders of his lover.

"Here's the fabulous Daniel."

Ken moved abruptly in front of me, hands outstretched. They exchanged warm greetings. At the precise moment I was about to include my own welcome I reeled with awareness I was looking at someone I had met before.

Not just fleetingly on a bus, either. It all came flooding back— as sharply defined as a Dürer engraving; almost choking me with the clarity of that encounter on the forward deck of the old passenger ferry which no longer plied the two-hour journey between the downtown port of Vancouver and its counterpart in Nanaimo. . . .

It had been one of those late February days, illicit elsewhere in Canada, when public and private gardens were already flecked with yellow crocus above which bold blossom waved from intrepid cherry trees. I had the car roof open since leaving Kitsilano but was still pleasantly surprised to find when I had chosen my spot on the deserted upper deck, that the sun was as warmly comforting as we sailed between the greening islands, as it had been on the mainland.

I was going to see our friend, Marjorie, who having played dutiful wife and mothered two children, had discovered in her forties that both had been first roles. She had fallen in love with a young woman lawyer and I was making my first visit since Marjorie had moved in with Phyllis.

As a house-warming gift, but part in jest, I was taking a copy of Simone de Beauvoir's The Second Sex *and was perusing its pages when I was approached and addressed by a young man.*

"I've always wondered which, exactly, the second sex is?"

At so much good looks and youthfulness I could only smile. "She doesn't lump men and women together under hetero-sex, if that's what you mean. Simone very much means women."

The gray eyes wandered lazily over me, my book, and my semi-hiding place, but right off the bat I sensed a sharp mind lurked behind that degree of beauty.

"Which makes any other sex third, I guess. Then that figures. Never more than an Olympic bronze—the third world. It's a pattern, isn't it?"

I was unused to frontal attacks—even verbal ones. Even those that were safely literary if one wished to make them so.

"In which case the third category would have to be a very large one. Or do you visualize a fourth, fifth and sixth? I shudder to think what that might be. Bestiality, perhaps? Or did you have something more exotic in mind?"

But he was through with the preamble. Madame de Beauvoir had served her purpose. "I saw you drive on the ferry. I came on as a foot passenger. I was hoping you'd come up here, away from the mob. Some place I could get you to myself."

"I'm flattered," I told him. And I wasn't lying. It was up to me, I felt, to be at least as bold as he.

"And what was the purpose of all this solitude?"

"I was attracted. You're my type. And as my taste in men is rare I have to grab while the going's good."

(As I recalled that statement my glance flashed between him and Neil. Either he was lying then or his taste had changed radically in the two years or so since that high seas encounter. Neil and I could not have looked more dissimilar!)

Without even casting about him he had suited actions to words and had lunged forward and nudged me in the vicinity of my genitals. Boldness in words was one thing—action quite another. As quickly as he'd moved to my fly I grabbed my raincoat and draped both my private parts and his enquiring fingers.

"Is this your usual thing?" I asked him. "To act like a praying mantis on the ferry systems?"

But I kept my voice genial. There was no denying I was flattered by the importuning from a handsome man—in spite of the imprudence of his aggression.

He grinned—not at all abashed.

"Sometimes," he admitted. "I'll tell you a secret. I've learned that if you want someone then you'd better act on the impulse or the opportunity will be gone. So the chances are that he'll tell you to fuck off. But for the nine who are rude there's always the tenth who's willing to take it from there."

"I should be destroyed by all that rejection," I said simply.

"A different temperament. It takes all sorts. But let's not waste time out here talking lifestyles." He nudged me harder under my raincoat. "You can do that anywhere and anytime."

With that we had proceeded to explore each other in a literally under-cover way. There had been elements of farce as we sat there behind the forward lifeboat pretending to look at the scenery as we sailed past Bowen Island, the foot of the Sechelt Peninsula, and, finally, the open waters of the Straits of Georgia.

By now the deck was no longer deserted. An elderly woman with a blue scarf tied in babushka fashion, to preserve the careful coiffure of her snow-white curls, plonked her large behind on a neighbouring life-raft and yanked a tweed-wrapped wisp of a husband down to her side.

"Why can't you enjoy nature like those two young men," she boomed over the wind (incidentally flattering forty-five year-old me) "instead of slobbering over every girl on board?"

"Because I'm feeling bloody cold," he'd spat back at his spouse. "I haven't got your fat."

With Daniel's hand plying expertly between my scrotum and prepuce, I, to the contrary, was feeling too hot—or at least, over-stimulated.

"Perhaps we should go down to the bar for a beer," I grunted. "I'm beginning to feel less and less responsible for what'll happen next."

But Daniel had been adamant, increasing his tempo and varying his manual techniques to the point I was wholly compliant and at the mercy of his fingers. I closed my eyes and would have stuffed my ears against her banal observations and endless war with her husband if it had been humanly possible. As it was she just faded from consciousness as I increased my forage into erotic realms by mutually feeling up my partner.

They had no sooner departed (possibly as a result of the kerchiefed woman noticing the peculiar movements under my raincoat) than they were followed by a teenager and his girlfriend. These two differed from the older couple only by it being the male who evinced interest in our clandestine activity.

They didn't sit down but continued to march the length of the deck. It soon became apparent that the ferret-eyed boy, dressed in a scarlet wind-cheater with a peaked baseball cap to match, directed their progress steadily closer to where we huddled.

Tearing my attention from the work in hand (as it were) I estimated that Mr. Curious and his listless companion would be smack in front of us by the second or third trip back from the aft end of the ferry. I was minded neither to meet his knowing leer or to have him nudge her at some tell-tale sign of our love-play—for I was perilously close to climax.

I exercised a degree of self-control I never realized I owned. "Come on," I gasped. "Let's go to the bar for a goddamn beer."

I wedged my thing back in its lair, hastily zipped up my fly, and escaped the confines of the spread-out raincoat which I donated Daniel as he strove to arrange himself in such a way as to appease public scrutiny.

When the scrawny youth drew side by side with me, I saw his sight flash down to my still engorged parts. But it was a look of hungry interest, not jeering curiosity which I read there.

It at once occurred to me that if my seducer were to suspect the kid's motives then, given the predatory manner he'd adopted with me, he might well seek to win him from his sullen-faced girlfriend who seemed as antipathetic to the sea breezes on the open deck as the skinny old man of the previous couple.

I swung immediately into action. "Let's pick up a newspaper on the way to the pub. That'll give us the ballgame scores. I never did see the finish of the Lions game on last night."

I might have spoken less loudly and with less confidence had I known then what my companion was to inform me a few minutes later—that the B.C. Lions had not played the previous night.

He appeared to bear me no grudge for aborting our sex-play but after chattering about nothing in particular and downing a beer in each other's company, he rose and made his excuses saying he thought he'd try a little more fresh air before we arrived in Nanaimo.

I thought he might still check out the scrawny youth with the unwholesome curiosity and so made quite sure I stayed right there in the phony Tudor surroundings of the CPR ferry pub, until the PA system distortedly blared out our destination.

Now, in our own living room, as I most assuredly encountered him for the *second* time in my life, I considered carefully the precise ordering of words I was about to employ.

"Haven't we met before, ages ago? On Vancouver Island? Nanaimo, could it have been?"

He not only shook his head but I saw nothing of recognition or stirring memory in those clear eyes.

"I don't think so. Though I'm sure I've seen Ken on campus."

I dropped it then and there. The look on Neil's face was too ecstatic for anything to be risked.

"Come to think of it, I remember now who you remind me of. It was someone who worked for the CBC in Toronto."

Perhaps a quick sign of relief flicked across the face of Neil's new lover, but that could easily have been my fancy.

"Don't you think he's terrific?" Neil asked. "Don't just stand there looking, Davey. *Say* something!"

Daniel took pity on me. "I think I have a conveyor-belt face. People are always thinking they've seen me some place. And I've only ever been a restorer in Vancouver, since my graduation from UBC."

I smiled. "I'm quite certain now I was thinking of John Lang. And the more I look at you the less like him I think you really are! The only thing you have in common are good looks!"

"*That's* what I want to hear," cried Neil—though it was more of a squeal than a shout.

"You shouldn't embarrass people by fishing for compliments on their behalf," Ken told his friend, laughing. "Serve you right if Daniel were to ask us what we thought of your ugly-looking mug!"

Daniel's response was swift. "Like I said, I'm a restorer of ancient material. When I met Neil I saw right away I had a challenge. Mind you, I only started while you guys were in Europe, so I haven't gotten too far!"

Neil led the laughter. In spite of being the butt of Daniel's sallies, he obviously revelled in the role of impresario for his lover's wit—as he was to demonstrate throughout the evening.

I was equally impressed by how his new lover seemed to brim with affection for our friend. The only hesitation I had over this radical eruption in Neil's life, was my suspicion that he recalled very well his experience with me on the CPR ferry but for reasons best known to himself, wished the past not only dead but interred.

When the two of them had departed and we were cleaning up and preparing for bed, I debated what I would tell Ken about that encounter on the Queen of Burnaby. I decided, finally, that I could hardly criticize Daniel for avoidance techniques if I wasn't prepared to level myself.

Even so, as I followed my lover upstairs, I ruefully acknowledged that in spite of the long years of togetherness, I still found it difficult to admit these chance encounters. The fact time had elapsed didn't make it all that much easier.

It turned out to be much smoother than I'd anticipated or than was usually the case. I had only just suggested I had met young Master Callaghan before—in spite of his protestations to the contrary— when Ken interrupted.

"That's funny. I've met him, too. On campus. Or to be more accurate, that's where I saw him. And in similar circumstances to those which landed poor old Neil in such hot water. I'd say they were birds of a feather."

Which was all a little too close to my own past proclivities for comfort. "He certainly wasn't about to admit we chatted on the ferry to Nanaimo even if it was some years ago. Perhaps they've agreed to bury the past and start afresh."

By this time we faced each other on adjacent pillows. "I hope so," Ken said thoughtfully. "Neil needs something solid to last him through if he's going to make such a big change in life a permanent one. In any case, I liked Daniel enormously. He's reassuring, don't you think?"

I agreed.

Just before we drifted off Ken added: "In spite of what Neil says, it could be awfully hard for his kid. It's tough enough for a straight guy to find out his father's gay—let alone come to terms with a second Mrs. Murphy who happens this time around to be a man!"

I said nothing. I'd already decided to sound my godson out and intended to do it without letting on to Neil, or worse, providing ammunition to an angry and disillusioned mother.

EIGHTEEN

≈

When I suggested to Benjamin, in late September, that we go together to Nanaimo to visit Marjorie and Phyllis, I swear I had no sense of symbolically repeating the ferry trip once undertaken with the sexually bold Daniel. But long before the car was moving up the steep metal plank to board I realized the significance of what I had done.

I felt stupid. There were a dozen projects I could have undertaken with the boy who was always happy to accompany me but this one certainly made any talk relating to Daniel difficult.

It was a different ship, of course, as the CP passenger ferry no longer existed. It was also a slightly different route as the government ferry left from a Horseshoe Bay terminal and berthed at another in Nanaimo. Nevertheless, I made sure we chose an alternative deck and determined we avoid any discussion dealing with the new *ménage à trois* of which Benjamin was now a member.

We had only just sat out on the patio of the ramshackle but comfortable beach residence that Marjorie and Phyllis shared when the subject was confronted.

"So, young man, how are you enjoying things now with your Dad and his Daniel? Settling down and adjusting?"

I relaxed. I could never have embarked on such a direct approach while remaining composed but I had guessed it was how my friend would act. That was the main reason I'd chosen her as catalyst—to get a full picture of Benjamin's current emotional state. Marjorie was the kind of crisp individual with a frontal approach that I have always regarded as a special gift of many lesbians. She didn't let me down now.

Benjamin spoke as if I were not there. That's to say he didn't vouchsafe me a single glance as he answered her.

"It's great, Aunt Marjorie, it really is. I don't remember Dad in such good shape. He's stopped bitching at me all the time.

"And I do like Daniel. He's real good for Dad. Doesn't let him get away with a thing!

"Dan lets me help out with some of his jobs and use his special preservative chemicals. I think I might go in for restoring, you know. He's promised to show me all the stages. Only he says I should go to some place for real technical training. He doesn't think I'm cut out for UBC to do stuff like English or history like Dad wanted me to. Anyways, Dan has now got Dad to agree with him. He said I can please myself when I graduate."

I stared out beyond where the ocher leaves of the vine interwove with those of morning glories around the trellis in the motionless fall air. I had not heard any of this before, although Ken had indicated it was Daniel who wore the pants in the all-male Point Grey household.

"And what does your mother think of all this?"

I looked back across the table in time to see my godchild provide a shrug so Gallic that even his grandfather would have been proud of him.

"You know what she's like, Aunt Marjorie. Now she doesn't have Dad to whine at, I get it all. To tell the truth, I hate going to stay with her—even though she has a special bedroom for me and it's a nice little apartment and that.

"She wants me to stay there most of the time—but when I do she's always bugging me about things—like schoolwork.

"It was bad enough when we were in Europe but it's worse now. Dad may have been persuaded about my not going to UBC but she sure hasn't! Not a day goes by when she doesn't bring it up. I told her what Dan says but she just goes silent. I guess she doesn't like to talk too much about him. She told me once she wasn't interested in anything he had to say to me."

I couldn't let him get away with that. "That's hardly surprising, is it, Benjie? I mean—put yourself in her shoes. First there was the shock of finding out about your Dad and Daniel—then her having to accept someone else taking over her home, her husband—even her son!"

"It couldn't have been a total surprise for her, Davey," Marjorie interjected. "God knows, we've been hearing about Neil's adventures since the beginning of time!"

"Mum has had her own things, too," her son volunteered. "It's wrong to think that everything's been Dad's fault. There've been times when I've come home from school at night—after band practice for example—and, well, Mum hasn't been there alone. I'm not a fool, you know."

"No one is suggesting you are," I said—with greater gentleness than I was feeling. "There's no point in trying to set up some kind of balance sheet between them. All I'm saying is that this is *not* the time for you to go all judgmental over your mother. It must be bloody hard for her—and you of all people should be aware of the fact."

Inwardly I was seething in defense of Jacqueline. When thinking of her in the context of Neil and his new mate, I fell easily into a towering rage—of which any feminist would have been proud!

Why was it invariably the woman left holding the marital ashes while her husband blithely recycled his aging genes on behalf of a fresh face on young shoulders? And the fact that in this instance she had been replaced by a younger male only proved how obfuscatory could be a bunch of labels.

Marjorie forestalled me—and did it without berating the kid or playing one parent against the other.

"I think what Davey means, Ben, is that your mother needs you particularly at this moment—much more than your father does with Dan to comfort him. She's not going to say as much, of course, because her pride's hurt. That's why she takes it out in nagging you a little over this and that.

"But you're a big guy now. You can surely keep one jump ahead of her, can't you? I think it would be great, for instance, if she doesn't have to always suggest you stay with her but that it comes from you."

"You sound like Aunt Helen! She's been telling me ever since we got home to be all grown up with Mum. That's pretty hard, though, when your mother insists on treating you like a kid all the time! Anyway, how did things work when Derek and I were really little? What did you people use for excuses then?"

That made Marjorie hoot—and by his impish grin I not only knew he'd intended her to, but that he was coping with the oddities of his new domestic circumstances in a manner I wouldn't have believed possible during our progress through Europe. I was ready to burst with pride for my Benjamin. . . .

By the time we returned next morning to the mainland he had me crying hysterically on the deck as he wickedly imitated both hooting Marjorie and her rotund companion, who rolled like a sailor as she weaved her great bottom between the furniture of their crowded living room.

NINETEEN

≈

He didn't get serious until Horseshoe Bay first hove into sight—and then it wasn't about his parents. He suddenly stopped clowning, pushed the hair from his eyes, flopped back on the slatted bench, and breathed out heavily—making a raspberry.

I thought that moment he seemed more twelve than seventeen. Then his mother had fondly observed on the trip, especially when the two boys had been playing on the beach, that in their adolescence they often offered flashbacks to childhood as they strove, like spawning salmon, to make one more jump up the river towards maturity.

I also recalled Ken suggesting that too many seeming adults had never made it—and wondering, nervously, to whom he might be alluding. . . .

The boy's next words put paid to that disquieting recollection—only to replace it by something more immediately in need of attention.

"I didn't think I was going to like Phyllis at first, but she's as nice as Marjorie, isn't she? Davey, why are they called dykes? And what's a dildo?"

I shot a desperate look at the coastline—which we couldn't reach soon enough for my purposes!

I stuck desperately with the etymology of 'dyke.'

"I'm not quite sure. I remember looking it up once but my dictionary only gave alternative spelling with an 'I' or 'Y.' Anyway, it's not a term I particularly like."

"Why not? Both Marjorie and Phyllis used it last night."

"That doesn't mean you should. You will sometimes hear black people like our friend, Roger, say *nigger*—but that doesn't give whites the right to do so. Minorities often use put-down words about themselves. Somehow it takes the sting out of being the butt of other people's unpleasantness."

"Like you and Ken calling yourself faggots?"

"Dead on. But I wouldn't like to hear you calling us that as you jolly well know!"

"What should I call Marjorie and Phyllis then?"

I didn't want to be pedantic—nor, God knows, to indulge the sarcasm which can stir at the slightest provocation.

"The same dictionary offers lesbians which comes from Greek mythology which you can check out when you get home if you haven't already."

"I don't think that would go down too well at school. I had enough trouble when it got around about Dad on campus. I sure haven't said anything about them splitting up. I did tell Ned Ince, though, that Dan was a cousin of Dad's who's come to stay with us for a while. Then he kept asking over and over. You know what a snoop he is—especially over things like that."

"It suggests he doesn't ask enough questions at home. His father is pretty closety and finds it hard to speak about a whole bunch of stuff."

"Like you, then?"

I glanced sharply at him. The little bugger looked wholly serious. I couldn't be sure whether he was having me on or not.

He was obviously in a mercurial mood if not a quixotic one.

"I haven't talked much with Derek since he got back from Villefranche. Boy, his family have *real* problems, if you ask me!"

For one dreadful moment I thought he was about to announce the separation of Helen and Gordon, but that was far from the case.

"Derek only wants to talk about Muriel and their plans but I know he's worried about a whole bunch of stuff."

"Such as?"

"Oh, you know. Like his father wouldn't stay with Dad when Dan arrived on the scene? He went back home even before he'd finished painting the apartment. Dan told me there was a real dust-up between my Dad and Gordon who kept on about marriage vows or some shit."

I thought at that moment Dan might well keep his mouth shut more often. What I said was: "For someone who's had a season ticket to the steambaths I think Gordon could be a little less harsh over other people. Then the trouble with puritans is they have difficulty in confining their morality to themselves."

I knew I was being disloyal to a gay friend before a straight youngster but the words just surfaced unbidden. Coming from Calvinist

Cornwall I'd early learned that to remain sane you either had to hate puritans or be one.

"He's given Derek a hard time, I know that, over Muriel. He thinks they shouldn't even write to one another! And he blames Helen for not being firmer when she went to see the Woolnoughs in Villefranche."

There was something about the enthusiasm in my godson's voice which I found off-putting. He seemed to be overly savoring the tensions in the Goddard family and I didn't like it.

"That's all very interesting, but you have your own problems to sort out in the Murphy camp. For one thing, I suggest you start by following Majorie's advice and get on a better basis with your mother."

That shut him up for a while but he got in a further shot before the bump of the ferry against the dock and the engine screws roared in reverse.

"I guess it's specially hard for families like mine and Derek's. Some people should think twice before marrying in the first place."

The drive back in the car was unusually silent. . . .

I arrived home to find Ken out at the university having left a note to call Helen which I did at once. I had striven hard to appear unconcerned when Benjamin had been speaking of the Goddards but I had registered all he'd said.

It was now late morning and she asked whether I could manage lunch. I agreed, especially on learning that Gordon was at work and knowing that Ken wouldn't be back until mid-afternoon.

I wanted intimate talk with her and prayed all the way to the apartment that Derek would be out too.

I was in luck.

She asked me into the kitchen as she rustled up a feta cheese omelette and I knew she was feeling warm towards me because that was what we had had one special day in Marseilles—when the boys had set sail and she was feeling blue and I had told her it was my favourite.

"Enjoy your trip with Benjamin? And how were Marj and Phyl?" Helen was the only person I knew who fore-shortened their names—then she did that with most people including her own son—whom she abbreviated all the way to plain 'D'!

"They were both in good form," I told her, "and were especially good with Benjamin. You would have approved if you'd heard them telling him to be a good son to his mother."

"I don't know how much either of them would know about *that*," she commented drily as she fished the feta out of a pudding bowl she took from the fridge. "But I guess we Mums should be thankful for all good advice handed out to our offspring from whatever the source. Talking of which, you might drop a hint to my pride-and-joy to stop pushing the virtues of his ladylove under his Dad's nose. Gordon will come around to anything—but he won't be bullied. You know how obstinate the gentle ones can be. Look at Ken."

As usual, it took a few moments to absorb everything Helen crammed into one of her longer utterances. I tried to start at the top and work down.

"In the first place I don't think that simply by being gay Marjorie and Phyllis are deficient in the quality of advice they can hand out to an adolescent about his mother. And of course I'll drop a hint to Derek if you say so—only I'm not sure he'll listen to me on the subject of his father. And finally—who the hell ever described Ken as *gentle*. I'd have called him tough as tungsten—and I should know. He's run my life long enough!"

"What on earth is tungsten? No—don't bother to tell me. I've got too much nonsense cluttering my head as it is—or so Gordon keeps saying. Tell me about Ben—and that odd set-up he's living in. How's he getting on with *Uncle* Daniel, alias the *second* Mrs. Murphy?"

"I will after you've told me about things around here. I gather your Hubby and Neil didn't exactly see eye to eye while we were away."

"And they say women are gossips! You can't beat a gaggle of queens, if you ask me! Would you mind breaking off enough of that baguette for the two of us?"

As I complied and dropped the segments into the straw *panier* she'd put out for the purpose I replied in kind. "No one is asking you, honey. And in this case, you've got it all ass-about-head. It was Benjamin who told me on the ferry—and I'll give you one guess as to where *he* got it from. I'll have to admit, though, that our dear Daniel is a bit of a yakker. There's something else, too, about him I haven't told. Only I shall keep that as bait until I really want something out of you."

Helen was too smart to start an interrogation. Then she could afford to wait. She knew me well enough to realize I'd volunteer any information if it wasn't eventually demanded.

"You still haven't said how Ben is coping with two fathers—or is it two mothers? It must have been quite a shock for him when he got home to find all that waiting!"

"He and Daniel get on like a house on fire, so if you try to sniff trouble in that quarter you'll be disappointed, luvvy. Neil and Danny-boy are mutually infatuated. All you hear when you visit is the creamy sound of violins!"

"You have to be asked first," she said, whipping the eggs with unnecessary force.

"Well, I understand Gordon rather put paid to that, didn't he?"

She dribbled olive oil into her salad bowl. "Gordon does what he feels he has to do. I have no say in it."

I was about to inform her I was well aware of the fact but thought better of it. Helen hadn't asked me over there to merely gossip about the Murphys—nor to trade quips about her husband.

As soon as we had both traversed the serving counter and put the salad and cheese omelettes on the already-laid table, she unburdened herself.

"He's still not himself, you know. He'll tell you he is but it's simply not true."

I helped myself to lettuce.

"The business with Neil and Dan, his erupting over Derek and Muriel—it's all to do with himself really—and his—his, well, lack of self-esteem is what his shrink called it when I spoke to him."

We looked across the expanse of teak tabletop at each other. The dining nook and living room beyond it seemed very empty: desolate even, in spite of a cheery sunbeam cast low across the biscuit-coloured carpet.

"The closet can be a hard thing to get really free of," I said carefully. "It's been harder for Gordon than most."

She grimaced. "Depends how you look at it. In one sense he's been out so long there's cobwebs blocking the way back. He's not exactly been playing Tarzan in bed with me since Derek was born. But if he had a child for every time he's been screwed since you and I met on the ferry, he could have brought Vancouver's population up to Toronto's by now! He must be a walking colander!"

I wanted to smile at her hyperbole but looked at my oozing feta instead.

"You could always do a Jacqueline."

"Leave him? Why on earth should I do that?"

"You tell me. He's your husband—not mine."

"What I will tell you is that he's a damn good father—better than I'm a mother if it comes down to it. And he's a bloody sight more conscientious than lots of husbands I know. If it were not for all this 'I'm a second-class human-being' business—"

She broke off. "No, Davey, I wouldn't dream of leaving him. Or he me, for that matter. He's no Neil, you know! And sometimes I give him an excuse to pick up and quit for reasons which have nothing whatever to do with him being gay."

"It seems to be catching. A kind of emotional measles," I suggested.

"What's catching?" She eyed me with intense suspicion. Then she was always so fucking protective over her Gordon—even when she started a discussion involving him and his problems.

"Self-denigration," I said pertly. "You're as good at it in your own way as he is. Maybe that's the secret cement of your marriage. Just like Ken being a masochist and me needing someone to worship is the secret of ours."

She laid her fork very slowly to rest. "Jesus, Davey! I know you're usually full of bullshit but I've never seen you this full before. And at midday yet!"

I bowed my head modestly. "For you, dear lady, I'd start as early as breakfast! Only what you call b.s. I'd describe as *home truths.* The real point is we have a lot in common. Which is why I'm here in the first place don't you think?"

She smiled at me and I knew with relief my slightly daring words had not been lost on her.

"Did you think I was going to explode?" she asked, grinning. "You don't have much faith in your friends!"

She settled to her purpose. "Of course I know I'm my own worst enemy. But that doesn't always help. People go on and on about self-knowledge but it's no good unless you're able to put it to use. I'm so weak. I can see myself charging in a certain direction—and know I can do nothing about it. That's where Gordon comes in. He's much more nimble. He can either dodge out of the way or think up some solution before I really do damage to all three of us. Mind you, we're not talking Hollywood Marriage here. On a scale of ten, Gordon is able to prevent a row, or halt one, about two times! For the rest it's mayhem—gore and tears with at least one of us slamming out of the apartment. It used to be mainly Gordon but it is becoming Derek more and more. And I don't like that one little bit."

I pondered all that. Or tried to. She'd touched on so many areas where I felt unqualified to speak. I decided to begin where she ended—with Derek. It was with him, after all, I now nursed a special bond since the promise I'd made to him that night in the village of Randanne.

"You musn't get Derek mixed up exclusively with whatever there is between the two of you. After all, he's at an age when rebellion is second nature. He might easily be slamming doors and walking out if his parents were screwing regularly and his Dad was as straight as Attila the Hun."

"I thought you guys claimed Attila, too, as one of yours."

"Shut up and listen! Derek can sort things out for himself—only he needs air to do it in. I think both you and Gordon get too involved. You shouldn't try and compete for intimacy with him. That's half the problem, if you ask me."

"I wasn't aware that anyone was. However, I am his mother. I know he respects you an awful lot, Davey. But you aren't his parent."

"You told me that on the way to California when Derek was still a little kid, remember? We'd just left the Oregon Caves—or was it at Fort

Ross—anyway, you gave me the same maternal message about not butting in."

"If you remember the location it's a pity you don't act on the message. I'm still his mother, you know, whatever he might say."

"What's that supposed to mean?"

"He told me as soon as I caught up with him in Villefranche that you'd promised not to tell me you'd met in the alley and he told you where he was heading. And I must say he informed his father, too, without any prompting from me, when we got back home."

"I must mention his name down at the CBC. The boy obviously is cut out for a job in the media, he's so good at spreading information. I suppose he didn't bother to provide the context in which I promised not to tell you where he was going?"

"Was it terribly important? As important as leveling with his mother? I told you he made it perfectly clear what he thinks of you—Ken, as well, come to that. Not by a single word was he disloyal to you. I overheard him tell his Dad that he thought you were the finest guy he knew. He even defended Neil and that Daniel when his Dad and I told him what we thought of the way they'd both treated Jacqueline."

I was about to retort hotly that I had made it perfectly clear to her son where my priorities lay, when I suddenly realized that would only be self-indulgence.

Telling her what a good boy I'd been at holding to my side of the bargain with Derek wouldn't help at all. Nor would I be relaxing strains in the Goddard family by recalling her son's rebellion in the car or by insisting on how ridiculous I thought Gordon's moralizing over Neil was—especially when his lofty attitudes had nothing whatever to do with Jacqueline and her unenviable situation. It was only the gay factor that obsessed Gordon—now as much as when I'd first met him.

"I'm glad that all got cleared up, then. I really did hate doing anything that smacked of being behind your back as parents. It's not the way Ken and I choose to go—with either Benjamin or Derek. And I guess over Neil and Jacqueline we will have to differ. We see the situation from different standpoints."

"You might talk to Jacqueline sometime. I'm pretty sure she'd appreciate that."

It was something over which I had had a gathering guilt for some time. I told Helen almost fiercely that such was my intention.

"But I didn't ask you here to talk about the Murphys."

"Nor about Derek, I presume."

Helen poured me tea. "Nor about Derek."

"That leaves Gordon."

"It also leaves me."

"I'm sorry. I didn't—"

"Doesn't matter. In fact I was thinking of Gordon *and* me. What I really wanted to tell you is that he and I are closer than when Derek and I left for Europe."

"A sort of opposite situation from Neil and Jacqueline?"

"If you like. Yes."

"Does Gordon know all this?"

"Clever bastard! He doesn't always speak about things. But I know he feels very close. He's quit going out at nights, you know."

I sipped at my cup before shaking my head.

"No, I didn't know. I'm glad for his sake, though. That always made him feel worse, he told me."

"He's given up booze as well while we were away. Mind you, that was never a problem after the breakdown."

"Well, he'd already given up smoking when I did. What vices does he have left? We all need some—otherwise there'd be no need for Lent!"

"Smart-ass! You know how much he loathes himself—that's surely enough for him to cope with."

"My dear Helen, that isn't necessarily so much a vice as a self-indulgence."

"Not with him it ain't!"

The grimness of her tone banished any further levity on my part. Like it or not, I was going to have to face whatever it was she was determined to present for my consideration.

"It's a sort of religious thing. Knowing your background I thought you might be able to understand. That was something else he and Neil fought over. You know how Neil can be. Remember Ben's baptism! Neil apparently caught G. watching one of those religious TV shows on a Sunday morning and started to laugh at him. That's when G. brought up the business of Neil deserting Jackie for some trick he'd picked up on Wreck Beach."

I sighed. "It wasn't Wreck Beach. It was the tie department at the Bay. And I don't know who deserted whom—considering it was Jacqueline who left with Benjamin for Lyons and her parents—and hadn't even decided whether she was ever going back to him."

"Let's not get into an argument over that, Davey. It's Gordon's involvement with all this religious stuff that's worrying me. We now get *Plain Truth* delivered in our box regularly and he not only watches all those TV evangelist shows but he's written to them as well. We get all their junk in the mail, too."

"But you said he was much better than when you left?"

"Much better. His shrink says he's made extraordinary progress and of course, he was able to go back to work after all that time. It's only all these Fundamentalist programs he watches by the hour. He's even found those which show on weekdays."

"I remember how it was that afternoon at our place when he kept making all those religious references. His family background—that was some kind of sect, wasn't it?"

"Plymouth Brethren. But by the time we met he was cut off from his family. There was only his father left, and he was gaga in some geriatric ward."

"Let's hope it isn't all surfacing from some place where he's suppressed it over the years."

"Not according to his psychiatrist. I specifically asked him about that, too."

"Have you discussed it with Gordon?"

It was her turn to shake her head.

"He won't. He just changes the subject as soon as he can. Mind you, he's very polite. Nothing about minding my own business or anything like that. In fact he'll change the program for one I want. But then I see him turn to one of the tracts he's been sent."

"Perhaps it's all genuine," I suggested. "Perhaps he's being converted."

"Do you believe that?"

"Weirder things have happened."

"That's no answer."

"But if it's true, what would you do about it?"

She leaned across the table towards me. I don't think I'd ever seen Helen look more earnest—or perhaps I should say more desperate.

"I'd go along with him. I love the guy. I intend to keep whatever we've got in one piece."

"You mean you've no intention of ending up like Jacqueline."

"I intend to keep our marriage intact. We're not kids anymore. Derek will be fleeing the nest sometime—this year, next year. With Muriel or whoever. Frankly, I'm brighter than Gordon. I've got to do the thinking for both of us. A little religious hypocrisy on my part is a small price to pay. Don't forget my background as a bloody Baptist. It would be an easy role for me to play. I sure know the lingo!"

That was the first time I'd ever heard Helen admit she might be superior to her husband in any respect—though, God knows, she acted on the assumption often enough!

"You're one smart human being, my friend!"

I stretched out my arm and our hands clasped to the left of the Michaelmas daisies she had placed between us.

"You don't think I'm a scheming bitch, then?"

"If so, thank God for S.B.'s. The world needs more of them! Especially ones in mixed marriages with a gay partner!"

"There's nothing particularly special about ours. Every marriage has its peculiarities. Surely even you and Ken realize what you two have is different from other gay couples?"

"Now who's full of bullshit! I can't count the number of times I've heard you argue that marriages involving bisexuals are the toughest to sustain. And that you and Gordon have had to make up your own special rules—particularly since Derek came along."

"I've never claimed to be consistent. Nor have you, for that matter. I thought that was one of our bonds."

She had me there. I couldn't help echoing her smile—however dolefully.

"Is that why I like you? There has to be some very esoteric reason—especially when you insist on giving me a hard time."

"Talking of which—would you like some of my lardy cake? I'm afraid it's hard because I left it too long in the oven."

"Your lardy cake, my pet, I would eat if it were *fossilized.* Even Jacqueline loves it—and you how when the French talk about *le cake* they make the word sound like 'ka-ka'!"

While she was busy at the counter cutting the dessert into fingers and placing a scoop of ice cream alongside on the plates, my mind turned to the absent Jacqueline. Helen had indicated she hadn't seen her friend for some time and I wondered if the different fate of their marriages had something to do with it. I told myself, if I were Jacqueline, I wouldn't necessarily want constant reminders of what *had* been—at least in terms of worldly goods and physical comfort. For the Murphy home had most certainly been comfortable and she had never seemed less than enthusiastic in the role of faculty wife and mother.

Come to that, with both women, in spite of a sharp nod towards women's liberation, there was no evident inclination for freedom from marriage or desire to take a paying job outside the home. To the contrary, they had both grown angry when I'd suggested that, with the kids growing up, they might consider such possibilities.

Helen had merely snorted and informed me she had already given her best years to the partnership with Gordon and that was how it was going to stay until death did them part.

Jacqueline had taken a different tack. After pointing out that Benjamin was younger and still needed her physical presence, whether he was aware of it or not, she pointed to all she did as a volunteer worker in the Point Grey area and argued that such activity was vital and should never be left to professional employees of the city or province.

I vowed to bring all that up when we next met—which turned out to be rather sooner (after devouring every scrap of Helen's lardy cake before departing) than I had intended.

TWENTY

Jacqueline. I ran into her along the seawall encircling Stanley Park. No, that isn't quite accurate. I saw her—from the back. She was several yards ahead of me but I could never mistake that toss of mane and the quick step. Besides, I heard her suddenly shriek with laughter and no one on earth sounds quite like Jacqueline when she erupts in mirth.

In conjunction with my recognition came the realization she wasn't alone. I slowed down. She was with a young man whose blond hair came part way down the back of the pink sweater he wore.

His laugh was as loud as hers—though slightly higher pitched. They were evidently enjoying something they found very funny. I absorbed that. So Jacqueline wasn't spending every minute of her life eating her heart out. . . .

They were now approaching the section of the path near Lumberman's Arch—opposite the rock on which the mermaid perched. It was just at the turn I was able to glimpse her companion's profile. It looked familiar but I couldn't place it. In spite of my conviction over meeting Daniel first on the ferry, it was not the first time I cursed my poor powers over putting a name to a face.

A few yards further down the almost deserted path—it was still quite early on a Saturday morning—it occurred to me I was in fact spying. I could've easily passed them (my purpose, after all, was to exercise by brisk walking) but I felt strangely reluctant to do so.

I wasn't quite in a position to eavesdrop but a breeze was blowing back from them and their conversation was sufficiently loud for me to catch distinct sentences with very little straining.

I was particularly intrigued when I detected references to both Benjamin and Derek from the young man and then clearly heard my friend firmly state she knew there was nothing romantic between the two.

I felt it expedient to catch up.

"Did I just hear my godson's name taken in vain?" I enquired lightly. "And what might you be doing out here flirting with a young man at the crack of dawn?"

"I might ask the same of you!" Jacqueline retorted. "Were you cruising in there among the ferns?"

Her comments seemed far more declamatory than mine. I hastily changed the subject. "Perhaps you'd better introduce us. I wouldn't want your young friend to be embarrassed."

"Introduce? Oh come on, Davey! You're the one who should feel embarrassed. You don't have to be introduced to *Ned.* For God's sake—you've known him since—"

"Since Ben's baptism. Or so Dad loves to tell me when he's nagging me about getting a job. Of course, I can't remember. I was only the sweetest little tot at the time. Not that I'm as ancient as I must look at this revolting hour of day! Actually, I'm only a year and three months older than Derek Goddard—something he insists on telling me whenever we meet."

I felt several kinds of a fool. "Of course I recognize you," I said hurriedly as I cast around for confirmation of the fact. "Oddly enough, Ned, I thought I saw your double at the Étoile in Paris this summer—just before we met up with Jacqueline. Only Ken explained that you were with your folks in California."

The young man gave a theatrical shriek. "How right he was! And how I wish I had been in Paris! That's my spiritual home, you know. I was telling Jacqueline how ghastly it was to be in San Francisco with all that lovely temptation—but to have your parents tagging along! It was the biggest frustration of my life. Can you imagine? Getting the eye from this one and that—with my Dad spluttering in my ear about the way I was walking and asking whether I was wearing Mary's or Julie's perfume. The bitch!"

I felt at least one prayer had been answered when I recalled his siblings. "And how are your sisters? I suspect they didn't have the problems on the trip you did."

"Worse, according to Joan," Jacqueline interrupted, "then Freddy has all but given up on this number—compared to his sisters. Every day the poor man wakes afraid that one or other of them is pregnant!"

"At least he now knows I'm not likely to be *that,*" Ned chortled. "But when I first told him I was gay I think he believed anything could happen. He wouldn't have been surprised if I'd hauled some delicious black sailor hunk home for the night. Pity I didn't," he added as a rueful afterthought.

"You had no difficulty in coming out, then?" I asked.

I was playing for time. It was taking me a while to accommodate to all this up-front business.

Again, it was Jacqueline who answered me. "It was hardest with his father—wasn't it, Ned? I mean, Joan was like your sisters—she suspected you were gay even before you did."

I couldn't believe my ears. They appeared to have a depth of intimacy which I thought belonged only to us.

"It sounds as if all Vancouver must've known about you—with the exception of those two old queens in Kitsilano who, of course, learn everything late."

I glanced at Jacqueline who now walked between us as we approached the Royal Vancouver Yacht Club. "I don't remember you ever telling me you and Ned here were close pals."

"How could you? I never told you. Don't you remember telling me aeons ago it wasn't right to tell one person another was gay? Though Ben and Derek talked an awful lot about Ned in France and Spain. I'm amazed you didn't catch on. I found it so bloody hard not to interrupt them. They weren't very kind and, anyway, they got things wrong half the time."

Ned daintily plucked a leaf of oregon grape from the bank alongside him. "That's horribly depressing. If those guys don't understand—considering who *their* Dads are—who in hell is going to!"

That was something I felt I could speak to.

"It's a bit like cats and dogs," I suggested.

Jacqueline raised an eyebrow. "I thought that was to do with rain. Especially in Vancouver, no?"

"I was thinking of how perfectly at ease our cat is with our dog. They even sleep on the same blanket. But the minute Winston jumps the fence to chase birds and meets Lucy, our Dachshund neighbour, he goes into hysterical orbit. Ditto with Thor, the Elkhound. He loves Winston but if he sees a cat when we're out on a walk it's another matter. Different attitudes in the home from outside. Get it?"

"Rewriting *Aesop's Fables,* I see," Jacqueline said. "It's a great idea. What will you call them? *Gaysop's Fables*?"

Ned shrieked. "Why not *Davey's Gaybles*—that's much cuter."

I winced as I noticed the boy look quickly at me—presumably to see how I was taking the ribbing. I grudgingly gave him marks for sensitivity.

Besides, I was feeling oddly ambivalent towards Jacqueline. It was hard to put into words—it hovered between irritation and disappointment.

It wasn't just the discovery of her link with Ned Ince. Nor even learning she was accustomed to early morning walking—though our time together that summer had certainly not hinted at such.

It was more to do with her composure. I had been led to believe from both her son and Helen that she was broken-hearted and reduced to forlornly enduring the rubble of her marital life. But in this currently animated Frenchwoman, still chic in her early forties, I could discern no sign of the cuckolded wife or abandoned mother.

This was much more the Jacqueline who had spoken so dismissively of Neil when we were traveling, when both Ken and I had sought to soften her tone and, hopefully, to prepare for their reunion when we were all back in Vancouver. So much for *our* powers of persuasion, I thought sadly.

I grew aware of silence and sensed they were both waiting. "That's a brilliant notion, Jacqueline. But I prefer *your* title, Ned. Not to worry—some brilliant old queen will pick up the idea in the next little while and make a fortune out of it with a best-seller. You'll see."

"Ned wants to be a writer—why don't you ask Davey if he has any tips?"

I had no intention of bogging down in a careers chat with a smart-ass young gay, however sensitive. "You must come around to the house. Just give us a call and we'll arrange something."

Then I turned to Jacqueline. "I understand Daniel Callaghan has sparked an interest in Benjamin for restoring old manuscripts and things. Did he tell you, by any chance?"

I felt better. The ball was in her court and I'd turned the talk away from the two of them.

Only I had reckoned without the bond of their alliance.

"If that's what he wants to do, then of course I'm all for it. The only thing I shall hate is his leaving for the east when the time comes. It's the same for Ned. You're also determined to leave Vancouver, aren't you?"

The boy didn't answer immediately. I became aware of the clop of my leather soles on the hardtop. The other two were wearing running shoes. The sun was now a hurtful brightness over the Bayshore Hotel and the uncertain stream of slow-moving tourist traffic began to perceptibly thicken.

"I hate it here," Ned said sullenly, the gay brightness quite gone out of his voice. "Of course I want to leave. I shall suffocate if I don't. I loathe this small town atmosphere."

It occurred to me that although I knew who it was speaking so fiercely, even saw his parents from time to time and had news of young Ned on campus, periodically from Ken, I didn't really know him at all.

In the early days, when he had been a child along with Benjamin and Derek, I had had a sense of a well-mannered little fellow, full of grave charm. But then had followed a vital gap—from his early teens to the present. The full-fledged youth whom I now saw and heard was a total stranger with the opinions and attitudes of a world from which I was almost totally cut off. And I wasn't particularly disposed to like what I saw. Though, of course, my attitudes toward Jacqueline may have coloured my reactions towards him.

"There's nothing keeping you here, is there? I mean your parents don't have you under lock and key and it's a free country."

"Does that mean you've been talking to them? I know you like Dad but I'd always hoped that being gay, you wouldn't share his hatred of gays."

"Aren't you being a trifle ridiculous," I suggested. "I was merely pointing out the obvious. I get tired of hearing people bitch Vancouver when they can fuck off whenever they please. What does that have to do with my attitude towards your father and his hang-ups, let alone my sense of you?

"And if you're accusing me of homophobia I suggest you see your psychiatrist before leaving town. The trouble is you kids don't have a clue as to what real gay hatred is! I suspect your father is really only worried about you as his son—not as a faggot! One day you'll maybe learn life isn't quite so neatly black and white."

I did not try to make my comments friendly. In fact a whole lot of frustration was being channelled through my rebuke. Even so, his response was as instant as it was excessive.

"Jesus Christ! Another one trying to pull rank with his goddamn years. I'm not staying to hear that crap all over again from you. I'm sorry, Jackie—but I'll see you when we aren't going to be interrupted."

Before there was time to even mildly remonstrate, he was off, running ahead of us, his blond hair dancing crazily below his neck.

We watched him disappear around the bend.

"You shouldn't have been so harsh," Jacqueline said. "He's in quite a bad way. His parents are worried stiff."

"I can see why. Believe it or not, I was only trying to help. Frankly, there's something about our Ned that rubs me up the wrong way."

"Which is very odd—considering the patience I've seen you show with both Benjamin and Derek."

"Meaning he's gay and they're not?"

"Well, isn't it?"

"If only the world were as pat as all that! In any case, they don't go in for these flouncy exits. Or comparing me with their parents, for that matter."

"That's because they know you. It's obvious he hasn't a clue!"

With the younger element departed we slowed our pace. A little further on, where in summer cricket was played, I suggested a short-cut back to the car. I was sick of walking in the park.

As we moved across the short grass, still bleached from the rigors of the August sun, I finally answered her.

"Although we are always protesting about being caricatured over weak-wrists and lispy voices, we too often generalize about ourselves. I mean, if I ask myself what do I have in common with Ned Ince, how much is there beyond the gay thing? I'm almost the same age as his father but emotionally I've far more in common with you than him!"

Jacqueline nibbled her lower lip as she thought her way over the grassy hillock and then down towards the car which I'd parked near the zoo.

"You're taking it too far. Sure, he could be your son. Sure, like the boys, he grew up here and doesn't have our way of looking at things. But it stops there. For one thing he's very bright—like you."

I grinned. Would have bobbed a curtsy but thought better of it. "Thank you, darlink," was what I said instead.

She ignored that. "But it's more than both of you being smart. He shares something else that's hard to pinpoint. Ken has it too. So does Neil. I can't say it about a whole lot more because I don't know that many. You're all quick to take offense for one thing. For another—well, you can all be quite bitchy when you want to. I think it's that which makes a lot of people a bit afraid of being in gay company. You can be so cruel—perhaps without knowing it."

I stood there at the door of the Peugeot before I unlocked it.

"That's the negative list. Is there a positive one or are you just a masochist?"

"Of course I am," she said pertly. "I wouldn't have lasted as long as I did with Neil otherwise, would I?"

"Let's keep that to later," I suggested, as I opened her door and bowed her inside.

"Where we going?" she asked as I headed for the causeway and Lions Gate Bridge. "This isn't the way to Fourth Avenue."

She had already invited me back to her place but I'd refused, saying I had a few items of shopping to do for Ken and a dinner party that evening. The truth was I wanted to obliterate the past forty minutes by taking her to some quiet, open-air place which we had shared in the past.

"Remember the time we took Benjamin fishing at the lake with the kingfishers? Beyond Deep Cove towards Indian Arm?"

"What an old sentimentalist you are! That's something else you have in common with young Ned—only he talks about places we visited together two years ago rather than nearly twenty!"

I got into the right lane to head towards the North Shore. "You really do know one another, don't you?" I mused. "You'd better be careful or they'll be locking you up for kidnapping!"

"It isn't like that, idiot! It's just that he finds it easier to talk to me than his mother. That Joan Ince is second cousin to an iceberg."

I grimaced. "So you're playing surrogate mother? Who are you kidding? You think I didn't notice the way you looked at him? Besides, do you think he allows his mother to walk with her arm around him?"

We were now speeding over the Lions Gate Bridge.

Perhaps it was the notion of buoyancy, or the sense of expanse—from the Pacific waters far below to the sun-struck canopy of cloud pushing hard against the coastal range of mountains ahead. Whatever it was, Jacqueline suddenly opened up.

"I've never denied I'm fond of Ned. I will also admit—and if you laugh I will kill you!—it's more like having the daughter I've always wanted. If you want to throw in a whiff of something more—romantic affection perhaps, then you're welcome. It will never be more than that. What's more, Ned himself will never know of it. I'm not a blithering idiot—only a masochist as you're so fond of telling me. I mean, I'm not entirely unaware I'm a middle-aged woman and he's a sweet young, rather nelly, queen. So you can stop playing the jealous suitor! Have some pity on us poor fag-hags!"

I found her hand which was cold and held it tightly. I had not a single word to say. Her candor wiped me out. She still stared ahead with unusual concentration, even if she did change the subject.

"I suppose you and Ken have been to the house recently. Have they changed things much?"

"Not really. But why don't you go and find out. I understand you and Neil talk regularly on the phone. I know for a fact he'd love to have you visit more often."

"I—I don't have the energy. Or the skill to walk on eggshells. Nor does Dan, so I am sure we would end up hurting each other. I'd hate that. It's all right for Neil, of course. He just ducks away from anything potentially unpleasant. Then when didn't he?"

I couldn't let it rest there. "But you are being so passive, Jacqueline. That's not you."

I wanted to say, 'Where's your French dander, girl!' but after her confession a peculiar prudence held me in check. I knew I had to skirt gingerly around such a raw topic as her being ousted by Daniel Callaghan.

"I suppose it must look like that. But I told you in France that I still hadn't made up my mind about returning to Neil when we got back. Although that was more in terms of protecting Benjamin from scandal than anything else. So Neil took the matter out of my hands by meeting Dan. It's not such a big deal, you know."

"But you could've stayed there with Benjamin. I think most people would have said it was up to Neil to move out if he wanted to live with Daniel."

She smiled fleetingly in my direction. "Since when have the likes of us listened to 'most people'? Neil gave me the choice and my decision was to move out and take a small apartment. The only thing is that I didn't realize how small Killarney was—or think my son would be so reluctant to visit his mother and stay overnight."

She spoke lightly but she couldn't fool me. I knew all the tell-tale signs—from the tightening inflection of voice to the nose wrinkling, even the tapping toes! I may have stumbled across secret sides of Jacqueline that morning but it didn't obliterate the proven icons of friendship. My taking up the cudgels on behalf of my godson was a reflex action. She knew it, of course, before the words were fully out of my mouth.

"Darling, I know it's tough for him. But it is hard on all of us. And I don't just mean Neil and me. For Daniel too—even if he is more skilful at covering it up. This may surprise you, but I really like Daniel. As a matter of fact, I think I would get on with him better than Neil nowadays. I only wish I could get to know him better."

We were now escaping the abrasive neon and pennant-flapping ugliness of Marine Drive. I could drive more quickly between dun apartment houses which themselves gave way to industrial parks and finally splotches of countryside.

The change of scenery seemed to alter both our moods.

"How's Ken?" she asked conversationally. "Is he still happy teaching? And does he enjoy himself at home with you around all the time?"

I wasn't used to conceptualizing my lover let alone taking his emotional temperature. I was more prone—in response to enquiries over him—to offer data as to what he was up to on campus or provide statistics as to musical events we'd attended or books he was currently reading.

"He always likes the new academic year," I said. "You know how much he loves teaching. He's got a new senior course this year and is on the usual number of dreary committees which he loathes."

"I wasn't thinking so much of Professor Bradley as of your lover," Jacqueline said carefully. "There were times on our trip when I thought you were a bit—what shall I say—tetchy with him?"

I carefully nursed the steering wheel. "Oh, I don't know. More than most lovers who've spent over twenty years together?"

"I don't know anybody else who has spent that amount of time with someone else. Except my parents and they aren't exactly a good example as they scarcely speak to each other!"

"No one can accuse Ken and me of not doing that!" I retorted. "We even get laughed at for yakking all the time."

"What about sex?" she asked. "Do you still have much of that?"

It was fortunate I had both hands on the wheel as I might well have verged onto the shoulder. I would have loved to tell her not to be personal, but I couldn't. Not after what she'd told me on the bridge. Besides, it was simply not the coinage of our friendship. For the thousand things I'd wormed from her, if I now displayed prudery she would only heap scorn. I could lie, of course. But in the oddest way, it would have been easier to lie to Ken than to either Jacqueline or Helen.

I sought refuge in prevarication. "What an odd question—coming from someone who never even mentioned she was regularly seeing the son of an old friend of mine or telling me the kid had turned out to be gay!"

That didn't faze her for a moment. Instead she held up her splayed fingers, and started ticking them off with the other hand.

"Number one. I already explained I didn't tell you about Ned being gay because you'd drilled into me it was a lousy thing to do. Number two. Who said I was *regularly* seeing Ned? And number three. Since when have you been describing Freddy Ince as 'an old friend'?"

I saw, even before she was through, that I'd lost that battle.

"You're not going to waste two whole fingers, I hope!"

She laughed. "Not for a moment! Number four. If you've forgotten lecturing me about keeping someone's homosexuality to myself perhaps you've also forgotten when we swore like schoolkids not to hold secrets from each other. Only we then said it wasn't kid stuff but important to our relationship."

I hadn't forgotten, of course. Which was precisely the problem. "That still leaves you with number five," I proposed lamely.

"Back to square one. Do you and Ken. . . . It's important. I don't just ask embarrassing questions, you know that."

I drove in silence, past a wooded Indian reserve which was full of shadows and moisture from the mists of the fall morning.

She persisted. "If it helps at all, Neil and I hadn't had sex for ages. I've talked to other women, too. They say the same. There seems to be some great myth—promoted by Hallmark Cards or someone—that sex just goes chugging along in middle-age marriages. In fact it's a pile of crap!"

It wasn't hard to guess who, at least, one of her 'other women' was. Gordon had told me years ago he'd stopped having intercourse with his wife when he'd started going regularly to the steambaths.

It was then I thought I could perceive the pattern of her thinking—whether all-gay couples (or all-straight ones, for that matter) had a better time of it than the likes of her and Helen.

I had a rush of affection for her. "No," I said. "Ken and I don't exactly fuck very often any more. We *should*—but somehow we don't. At first—long ago—it was his fault. But ever since it's been really mine." I drew breath. "It's one of those things that didn't get talked about when it should and now it's gotten too big to be brought up. Funny that."

"So much for 'yakking all the time,'" she said thoughtfully.

We had reached the turn-off to our lake and as the bumpy surface required a degree of concentration on my part, I was able to offer a legitimate silence. My thoughts, though, were centered about the intensity of my love for Ken and of the obdurate chasm that so often froze the undeniable longing between us when erotic feelings threatened to turn into actual sex play. I wondered, like Jacqueline, if this were true of all aging couples and whether the great unspokenness was a kind of whistling in the dark as we approached old age and a successive shut-down of fucking functions.

Jacqueline was out of the car and standing on the shore confronting the choppy waters before I followed in her wake through a tangle of brambles. Dewdrops flashed in the sun across taut spiders' webs and a few swollen blackberries hung as tribute to a past summer.

Loons called in melancholy persistence across the lake. When I looked up to where she pointed, I, too, could see the pair of bald eagles circling in the blue rift amid the hurrying clouds. The lake was friezed with snow-capped mountains and I couldn't help thinking the scene would serve admirably for a poster as it contained every westcoast cliché beloved of the B.C. tourist industry.

Turning from the blunt-winged eagles, we stared fully into each other's face. Whatever we saw there wasn't spelled out. Perhaps it had something to do with a common vulnerability stemming from mutual confidences. At any rate, we both stretched arms to clasp each other as we kissed.

I had the fleeting thought of how wrong a stranger would be in striving to interpret our embrace. Jacqueline broke our clinch and took my hand in the more familiar Hansel-and-Gretel stance we usually adopted.

She suggested we make our way the few hundred yards to where we had long ago walked with little Benjamin in his bright yellow wellington boots and the school cap she had bought him in Dublin. He had proudly clutched his rod and line.

There, where the gravel at the lake's edge gave way to a grass bank, we sat down in the October sun and stretched our legs. This time we saw no kingfishers.